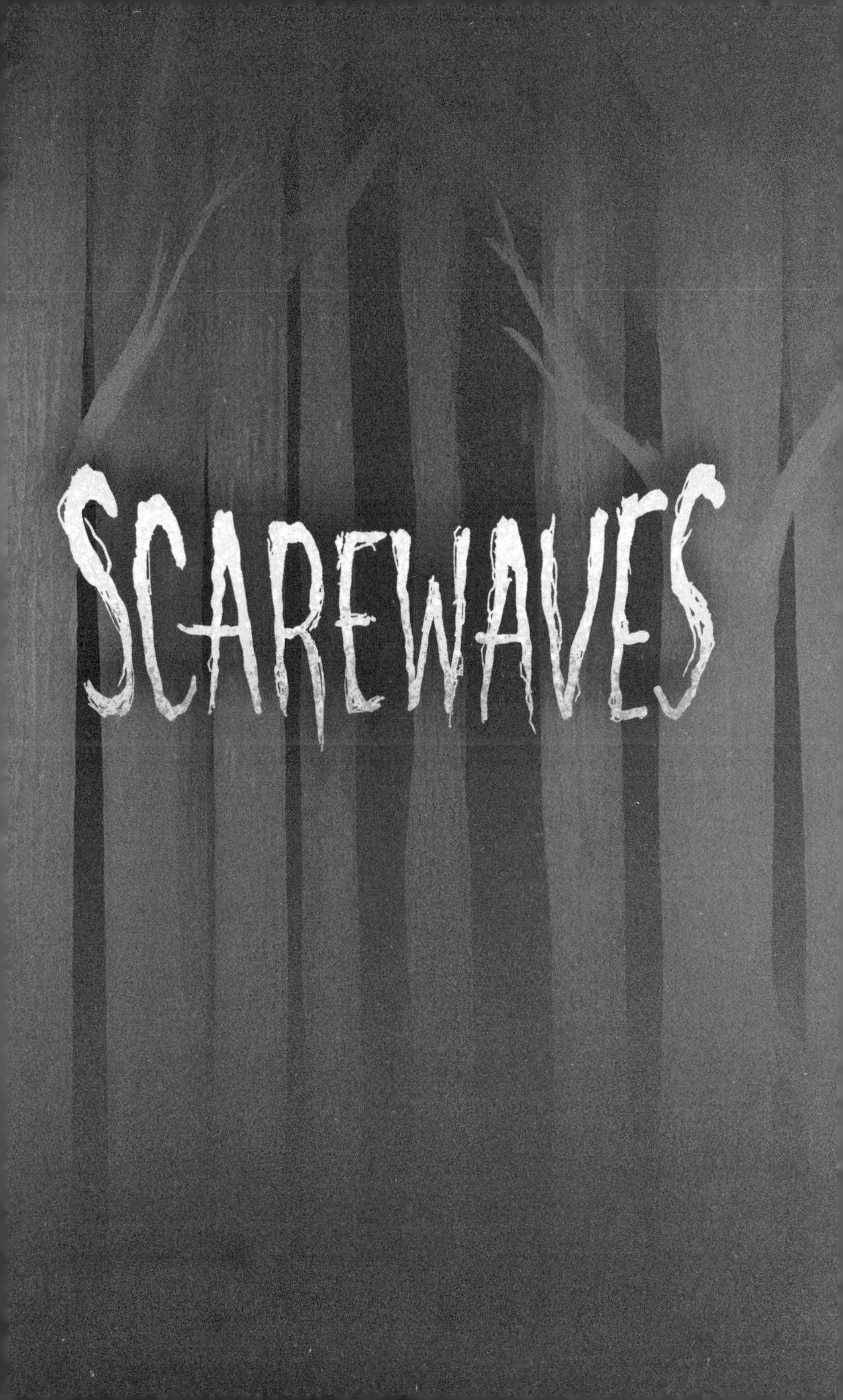
SCAREWAVES

SCAREWAVES

TREVOR HENDERSON

SCHOLASTIC PRESS · NEW YORK

All rights reserved. Published by Scholastic Press, an imprint of Scholastic Inc., *Publishers since 1920.*
SCHOLASTIC, SCHOLASTIC PRESS, and associated logos are trademarks and/or registered trademarks of Scholastic Inc.

The publisher does not have any control over and does not assume any responsibility for author or third-party websites or their content.

No part of this publication may be reproduced, stored in a retrieval system, or transmitted in any form or by any means, electronic, mechanical, photocopying, recording, or otherwise, without written permission of the publisher. For information regarding permission, write to Scholastic Inc., Attention: Permissions Department, 557 Broadway, New York, NY 10012.

This book is a work of fiction. Names, characters, places, and incidents are either the product of the author's imagination or are used fictitiously, and any resemblance to actual persons, living or dead, business establishments, events, or locales is entirely coincidental.

Library of Congress Cataloging-in-Publication Data available

ISBN 978-1-338-82950-1

10 9 8 7 6 5 4 3 2 1   23 24 25 26 27

First edition, October 2023
Printed in the U.S.A.   37

Book design by Christopher Stengel

FOR JENN, WHO HAS ALWAYS SUPPORTED ME.

FOR MY PARENTS, WHO ALWAYS ENCOURAGED ME.

FOR ALL THE KIDS WHO LIVE AND BREATHE MONSTERS.

AND FOR SCHOOL BOOK FAIRS, FONDLY REMEMBERED.

CHAPTER ONE
AFTER PRACTICE

Beverly Winslow picked at the mud that had dried between her soccer cleats. She was slumped on a cracked stone stoop with her coat pulled tight against her skinny frame, her bright orange knapsack beside her like a lump. Once a week, she put on her uniform, grabbed her sneakers, and started the long and gloomy walk to soccer practice at the Beacon Point Community Center.

The run-down building boasted a lush field out back, perfect for sports of all kinds. Bev loved sports, especially soccer, and despite the long walk, it was worth it to get to play with other kids, though it wasn't easy. Her parents both had busy jobs. They weren't around to give her rides, so it was up to her to make it to practice on time. Her friend Byron didn't care for sports, but he was usually there to watch. She always appreciated the support. This time, though, he couldn't make it, so she would have to endure the long walk home alone. Bev peered at the gray sky overhead, sighed, and brushed her brown hair out of her face. Today would have been a great day for a ride from her parents. Just once or twice, she would appreciate seeing their faces in the stands. They never seemed to make the time to come see her play, and it was finally starting to get to her.

Bev looked out over the cracked pavement and rusty chain-link fences from her spot on the steps. The road stretched off to the left toward town, and right, into the woods. The community center was perplexingly far from town, more on the outskirts. It always gave Bev an eerie feeling being alone out here. She was so close to the thick woods that surrounded Beacon Point. It seemed like they could close in around her at any moment.

Suddenly, the clouds above her broke open and a torrent of rain poured down. One minute a chill wind was blowing; the next, a wall of steady rain soaked her to the bone. Bev grabbed her knapsack and held it over her head as a makeshift umbrella, already off the stoop and jogging toward the road. It would be a miserable walk home through the rain, but she couldn't put it off anymore. The last thing she wanted to do was miss soccer practice next week because of hypothermia.

She was sure that by the time she got home, her mom would be there waiting to greet her. Bev left the parking lot behind her and started down the thin road that led to town. Rows of thick pine trees lined both sides, like two soccer teams squaring off. She shivered. Again, she wished that Byron had been able to meet her. The conversations they shared always made the trip go by so much quicker. By the time Byron finally ran out of steam talking about some new monster or ghost, they were usually at her front door. When Bev had to make the trek alone, like today, she brought an old Walkman that was a hand-me-down from her brother. The music made her focus on the walk and kept her from getting too creeped out. She untangled the cord hanging from her headphones, then slipped them on.

For a while the walk was calm. Her knapsack worked well as a makeshift umbrella, and Bev was content to lose herself in the music brought forth by the Walkman jammed in her back pocket. But then the song she was listening to was cut off by a blast of white noise, like a radio tuned between stations. Bev dropped her bag to the wet pavement with a yelp. She tore the headphones off her ears, yelling in frustration. "Stupid hand-me-down junk! I just want to listen to music!"

She was bending over to grab her bag out of a puddle when she heard a sharp crack from the woods directly to her right. It was the distinctive sound of a thick tree branch breaking. One didn't grow up in a wooded area like Beacon Point without knowing that sound by heart.

She paused, squinting to see between the trees, but the swaying pines formed a solid wall. Everyone knew that the Beacon Point woods were full of animals, especially out this far. It was always a good idea to avoid the forest at night. Bev shuddered. Suddenly, the feeling of eyes on her had real weight.

But the noise didn't repeat. There was no point standing around. She was still uneasy, but the rain was lightening up. Bev trudged toward home yet again.

Eventually, she saw the bent bus stop sign that told her she was about a quarter of the way home. The bus route had closed years ago, otherwise she wouldn't be slogging through this rain, but the sign stood as an indicator that she was making progress. Soon she'd be safe and warm at home.

"Bev-er-lyyyy."

A voice whispered from the woods, startlingly close. Bev stopped dead in her tracks, the air snatched from her lungs. She stared into the trees.

"H-hello?" she called, forcing herself to breathe.

The only response she received was the patter of rain against the forest floor.

She'd just about convinced herself that she'd misheard some other noise—an animal, or the sound of the dwindling storm—when she heard it again.

"Beverly."

It was just loud enough to reach her over the rustling leaves. The voice was raspy and harsh, but with an almost playful tone to it. A friend from soccer playing a joke on her, maybe? Or a kid from a rival team?

Bev took a hesitant step toward the trees, then another, crossing the muddy ditch that bordered the road and walking into the long grass. She stopped and listened. If whoever had called her name was still out there, they were being just as quiet as she was.

"Hey, creep!" she hollered. "That's really not funny!" She envisioned another kid standing just past the tree line, watching her from between the branches and waiting for her to get close enough to jump out and scare. Her skin crawled at the thought. Bev turned quickly back to the road—where a car blasted by in front of her!

Bev was sprayed with a huge splash of muddy water.

"Wonderful!" she yelled in frustration, the voice briefly forgotten.

Some parent must have been rushing back to town from Bev's practice, kids in tow. "Get a grip," she muttered to herself. "Pay attention, or you're likely to get creamed by a truck."

The rain had all but stopped. Only a light shower bounced off the rough asphalt. The sun was just starting to set—the orange glow behind the clouds meant night would fall quickly now. Bev tried to take a step back toward the road, but her left foot stuck fast. She groaned. Her foot must have gotten tangled in the long grass. If she ruined her soccer cleats by stepping off the road, that really would just be the perfect cap to this awful day.

Bev looked down, preparing for the worst.

Tragically, she found it.

A pale hand grasped her ankle. It was long and sinewy, with slender fingers broken up by thick, swollen joints.

Bev screamed, trying to kick the hand from her ankle even as it pulled her foot out from under her. She landed on her stomach with a crunch. Glancing frantically over her shoulder, she saw that the hand was connected to a long and slender arm, with skin as pale as the belly of a fish. It stretched out behind her into the darkness of the woods—an unbelievable, nightmarish length.

Bev suddenly caught sight of something across the road. Two

deer stood watching her, their imposing silhouettes distinct against the brush. She screamed again as the hand tightened its grip. The animals observed her struggle impassively, as still as statues.

They were the last things Beverly Winslow saw before she was yanked backward into the chilly shade of trees. With her final, desperate shriek, the road disappeared from view.

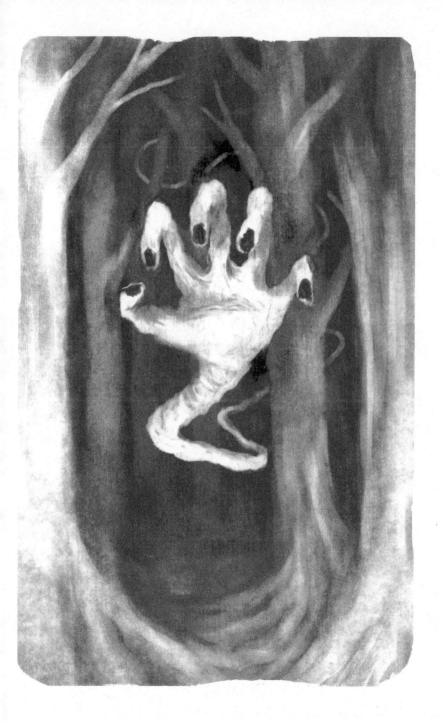

Ep. 03
"Beacon Point History"
Partial transcript of the
BCON RADIO MYSTERY SHOW,
hosted by Alan Graves

Broadcast on Jan 3, 1992

[Atmospheric spooky music plays]

[BG SFX: Lightning crashes, wolves howl]

ALAN GRAVES: Welcome back, constant listener, to a weekly dose of intrigue and truth, from me, your alluring and mysterious host, Alan Graves.

Tonight, I want to bring out the trusty grave-digging shovel and uncover some history. Some real history! Some Beacon Point history, which tends to be a lot more terrifying than the dusty, boring stories you'd find in most of your standard small towns. If we were to begin way back at the start of everything, we'd be here all night! But I'd be wrong not to acknowledge those strange lights, first and foremost. Most old-timers around here will agree, the lights have always been a part of Beacon Point. But what's unclear is whether they came along with the settlers, or if they've always been here. Some even say that they're the reason for the name, or that the founders chose this spot because the lights told them to. Since the beginning, Beacon Point has been an odd place. But honestly, the lights are the least of its problems!

[BG SFX: Lightning crashes, spooky laughter]

In 1878, the land that would eventually become Beacon Point was the site of many strange historical phenomena. On June seventeenth of that year, storm clouds rolled over the area, leaving a small rain of odd-looking bones in their wake, the smallest of which was only a quarter of an inch long. The biggest was almost a foot! No bones about it, that's odd. That's some skeleton humor for you, dear listeners.

By 1882, the first of many disappearances to come was recorded. An entire group of children on a school picnic disappeared into the woods and were never seen again. For months afterward, people who passed through the area claimed to hear children among the trees, their small voices crying for help.

In the early 1900s, rumors of odd wildlife and strange-looking plants started to circulate with the locals. In 1904, a group of hunters were attacked while pursuing a herd of deer. The sole survivor, an eccentric named Nathaniel Raymere, was found delirious and exhausted only a quarter mile from his home, ranting about animals with the faces of men.

Despite all the outlandish claims and missing people, some felt that the land was good for hunting and farming. And so, Beacon Point came to be. Whether this was a good idea or not is . . . still up for debate. If more people settled here, most felt, then that would be an end to the strangeness. But sadly, things only intensified. In 1910, there was an incident where the gathered townsfolk of Beacon Point witnessed a light that hung in the clouds over the town square for over three hours. Hundreds saw the light before it suddenly disappeared from the sky, as if it had never been there. Three of the witnesses were struck blind at that moment, and it was weeks before their vision returned. If you believe the stories.

In 1932, a hunting party recorded finding an abandoned campsite in the forests outside town. The tent was still set up, a fire still smoldering, but with no one in the area. Coffee brewed over the flames, and plates were laid out for a meal that never happened. Aside from the tidy eating area, the clearing was strewn with the belongings of whoever had been camping. The entire place was in disarray. The hunting party found the clothes of the missing men nearby, laid out on the ground as if the men wearing them had just disappeared into thin air, all lined up in a perfect circle.

In the early 40s, there were tales of a ragged figure, like that of a woman draped in layers of moldy garments, with the head of a monstrous crow. She was said to peer through the windows of family homes while they sat by the fire at night, kept at bay only by the light. Seeing the Crow Mother, as she was called, was a sure sign that misfortune would befall the children of those who lived there.

There have always been tales of bodies going missing from the local cemetery. Reports of folks seeing their recently deceased friends and family walking around their yards at night, asking to be let in. Doppelgängers, face-stealers, impostors of all kinds pretending to be those closest to you. But surely these are just fanciful stories, right? Right.

In 1973, one Abigail Ratchin was in her yard hanging up her laundry when a man walked out of the nearby woods. He was tall, dressed in a long coat and wide-brimmed hat that hid his face. He didn't come any closer, but Abigail said that

even from that distance she could tell
there was something wrong with his
proportions. And his smile. The way he
looked at her horrified Abigail, but
he stayed put where he was. So she calmly
went inside and waited for the man to
depart, turning and walking back the way
he'd come, right into the thick brush. But
for many nights after, Abigail claimed
that the Stranger somehow left threatening
messages inside her home, scrawled in the
hidden places on her property, in places
no one but she had access to. Eventually,
it was too much. Poor Abigail packed her
bags and fled Beacon Point in the middle
of the night, never to be seen again. Or
so they say.

Things in Beacon Point continued like this,
with a new strangeness every few years.
Monstrous animals in the woods. Ghosts.
Odd lights in the sky. People disappeared
more often than in neighboring towns, but
it was easy to look the other way, because
there were always more people moving in.
Most just wanted to go about their lives
unbothered. They figured if they kept their

heads down and stayed out of the woods, odds were they'd be just fine. That's how it is here. That's the BP status quo.

But I know I can count on you, dear listeners, to seek the truth. And the truth is that Beacon Point isn't just a place where people go missing, a place that has no shortage of strange tales, or where we stay out of the woods as a rule. It's also a place where people need to be careful what they say, and who they say it to. That's if they know what's good for them. Because in Beacon Point, someone— or something—is always watching, always listening, right along with you.

[Spooky outro music plays, lightning and thunder SFX]

We here at BCON Radio—and by "we" I mean "I"—appreciate you for being one of the rare few who doesn't know what's good for themselves. Or maybe you do, but you'd rather know the truth anyways.

Either way, thanks for listening. And as always, remember to stay safe, stay aware, and most of all, stay out of the woods. Good night.

[End of broadcast]

CHAPTER TWO

I ALREADY HATE THIS TOWN

Mary crossed her arms and sighed, both as dramatically as possible. She'd already read everything in the car twice over, and the boredom was killing her. The rest of her books were locked away in the big red duffel bag that took up most of their modest trunk space, as well as filling many of the big cardboard boxes in the moving van that was accompanying them to Beacon Point. There wasn't even any scenery to enjoy, as it had been raining for the last hour and all she could see through the backseat window was a streaky gray-and-green mess.

Mary adjusted her seat belt and tried to get comfortable. She'd been stuck in this car for hours and was almost completely sure she was getting a permanent butt cramp.

"We need to get there soon or I might actually die," Mary said. "I'm not joking at all. I *will* die of boredom." She depressed the button that lowered her window, letting in a little rain, before raising it again, keeping the car filled with an irritating electric hum.

Her dad rode in the passenger seat while her mom drove. They glanced at each other, then both turned to look at her, trying their best to hide their annoyance.

"Baby," her dad said, "we are *almost* there. You just have to hold on a little longer. Maybe a nap wouldn't hurt?" He sounded like he was on the verge of crying in frustration himself.

Mary didn't care. *They'd* dragged *her* to this dreary place against her wishes. She was allowed to be grumpy about it.

"I don't want a nap," she sulked. "I just don't want to be in this car anymore. And I *especially* don't want to be moving to some stupid new town." Mary made sure not to dignify her parents with eye contact, staring stubbornly again at the gray-green smear out the window.

It wasn't fair at all. She'd had friends in the city—favorite places, teachers she liked—and now she was leaving them all behind to go to some nowhere small town she'd never heard of. One day her mom and dad had just come home and told her they were moving. Say goodbye to everything you know and love, Mary!

She picked up an old magazine she'd already read and reread and re-reread during the long car ride here and flipped through it yet again.

"Honey, you're going to love it there," her dad said. "I know it was a sudden move, but it's really the best thing for me and your mom. And for you."

Mary's mom glanced at her through the rearview mirror. "We get that it's been rough, but I'm with your father. You just have to trust us." Her eyes flicked quickly back to the street, trying to keep her focus on traffic through the rain-drenched windshield.

In response, Mary shoved her face deeper into her magazine.

For a long while there was no conversation, just the sounds of the car and wind whistling through her cracked window, and the windshield wipers rubbing back and forth. Eventually, her mom switched on the car radio. A blast of static filled the air. Fumbling for the dial, her mom zipped between odd snippets of commercials and faint cheesy Top 40 hits before landing on a talk radio station. The signal came in especially strong, the host's voice quickly filling the car as if he'd joined them in person.

"As always, I'm your faithful guide through the eerie and the unreal, the macabre and the morbid, Alan Graves. Today I want to talk a little about our scenic town, our perfect little hamlet, and some of the more horrifying mysteries that have gone unsolved in Beacon Poi—"

But that was all Mary heard before her dad reached out and turned down the volume.

"Hey, that sounded cool!" Mary protested, but her parents were already pointing out something on the horizon.

"Look, Mary! See that?"

She peered at a structure that rose over the lush scenery in the far distance. The forest swept up into an intimidating peak that could only be the reason for the town name. Balanced on the edge was a squat structure that grew into an intimidating spire of metal, topped with a lone red glowing light. A radio tower? Maybe that was the workplace of the radio host they'd just heard. If he was that close, it would certainly explain why they were receiving him so clearly. Mary imagined him working away in an office at the top of that looming tower, churning out spooky stories and macabre facts.

Her reverie was broken when her dad suddenly clapped his hand on the dashboard excitedly.

"We're almost there!" he exclaimed. "Civilization!"

The first thing they saw was a lonely square building attached to a run-down parking lot and a small but neatly mowed sports field. It currently looked deserted. All the players must have gone home for the day. As they continued down the road, the thick

woods on either side enclosed the car in unbroken lines. Mary's attention was grabbed by a sudden patch of color off to the left, just at the tree line. A thin girl with long brown hair stood with her back to the road, staring into the trees as they drove past. She was soaking wet, despite the big, brightly colored knapsack she was holding above her head. They passed her just as she turned back to the road. Spinning around in her seat, Mary saw the car tires had worked up a regular tidal wave of ditchwater that splashed over the girl like a tsunami. Now extra soaked, she turned in shock to watch them go.

Sorry! Mary thought. The first person they'd seen in their new town, and they'd doused her with mud and ditchwater. Truly an amazing start.

Eventually, the thick foliage on either side of the car relented, with more and more buildings popping up. Mary saw lots of storefronts she'd never heard of before, no chains or franchises here. A small store named Video Wizard boasted a huge and weathered sign that took up most of the front window. It portrayed a stern-looking bearded man in a sweeping cloak. The video wizard himself, Mary guessed. A speech bubble in front of his mouth all but shouted: 5 TAPES—5 DOLLARS—5 DAY RENTALS!

Next to the business was a pizzeria, a convenience store, an ancient-looking bookstore, and a dentist, all wrapped around a shared parking lot.

Mary's parents pulled over briefly to get a few essentials from a small grocery store. While she waited outside, she spotted a butcher shop, a dry cleaner, and a few other storefronts nearby.

Back on the road, she saw a few businesses that went by too quickly to catch what they were selling.

Then, before she realized it, they were in Beacon Point's downtown area. So far, so normal—all very boring. The most interesting thing Mary saw was an ornate old-fashioned movie palace, its front entrance lavishly decorated. It perched on a side street with nothing but empty lots to either side of it.

In the distance, that peak loomed over it all, the radio tower stretching into the dark sky. It seemed to sway gently on the cool evening breeze, but Mary wondered if that was just an optical illusion.

Before long, they pulled up in front of their new home.

The house loomed above them—a massive collection of pointed angles that jutted into the evening air. It was a three-story Victorian that had absolutely seen better days. Her parents had apparently bought it for a song. They claimed that repairing their new home would make for a fun family bonding experience, but Mary eyed the house warily. She took in the decaying shingles and warped beams, and the cracked glass of a window on the third floor. This was going to take far more than a few weekends of work. Compared to their old place, the house was positively shabby, and not in a chic way.

In the end, they decided to leave the majority of their luggage in the car.

Everyone was an exhausted mess. The sky had turned a rich violet as the sun continued to set, and Mary could see scatterings of stars.

That's one benefit to living in a small town, she thought. *Way less light pollution, way more stars to see.*

Mary's parents carried in a few odds and ends, as well as their meager groceries. It would be another day or so before the rest of their furniture arrived, so all three of them grabbed their sleeping bags, pillows, and blankets.

After a thorough tour of the house (all old, all creaky), they made the living room their temporary home base and ordered a pizza. Mary assumed there was just the one place in town, and it had to be the place they'd seen next to the video store on the way in.

"Isn't this house beautiful?" her dad said. "Genuine hardwood floors!"

This was something he'd been repeating since they first started talking about the move, but Mary didn't get what the big deal was.

As she munched on pepperoni, she continued to take in their new surroundings. It was kind of cool how much their new place resembled a haunted house from a spooky movie. But that wasn't worth uprooting her life for.

Soon, they all finished eating and collapsed into their sleeping bags. It was still fairly early, but after that drive, Mary knew she'd have no problem falling asleep.

Tomorrow, she thought, already drifting off. *Tomorrow I can start on making this place slightly less horrible.*

Tomorrow the furniture truck would catch up with them and they'd arrange their new home. Mary would have to pick out a new room first thing, before her mom and dad got first pick of the best bedroom.

Unseen by Mary, crouched on the second-floor landing, something bent and strange looked on. Its eyes glinted in the shadows, its features moving and shifting as it watched Mary sleep.

CHAPTER THREE
MR. SACKHEAD

The dawn of the next day brought a sunny Saturday morning, but Lucas was already up. He ran a hand over his shaggy blond mullet while he brushed his teeth, his green eyes squinting in concentration as he inspected his long face, eyeing a new zit on his nose. He sighed in frustration and trudged back to his bed, falling face-first into the mattress.

Lucas rolled over and picked up the comic he'd been reading the previous night. Waking up early gave him some precious extra time to read or listen to music with the volume down to almost nothing, so as not to wake his father. He'd already taken care of the animals, but he dreaded whatever new chores his father had laid out for him today. There was always something new to attend to.

That was the trade-off if he wanted any time to himself. Lucas's father controlled every aspect of his life. Six days a week Lucas had to be up at the crack of dawn to tackle the long, *long* list of chores laid out for him, all in service of running the farm. Check on the livestock, feed the cows and horses, and then prepare breakfast for the both of them.

Sundays, at least, he was allowed to sleep in a couple of extra hours. And if Lucas was really lucky, he'd be spared a few more in the afternoon to work on the junky old car that sat on their property. He'd been tinkering with it off and on for years. By his estimation, it might actually be ready to go on some test-drives really soon, though he'd have to wait until he was old enough for a license to drive it on any public roads.

Lucas made his way downstairs and started breakfast. He'd

just finished frying a couple of eggs when his father groggily descended the stairs and pulled up a chair at the kitchen table, its legs scraping across the faded linoleum.

"Morning, Lucas," he said. "Animals taken care of?"

"Morning. And of course they are. I do it every day, don't I? I'm like clockwork!" But by then his father already had the paper open in front of his face.

A solemn "Sure, sure you do" rumbled from behind the classifieds.

"If you don't mind," his father added, "I have an extra little chore for you before you relax. I saw that our old friend Mr. Sackhead fell off his post last night. Be an absolute champ and go string him back up, will you?"

Lucas shuddered internally, but he thought he did a pretty good job not letting his father notice. He slid the spatula underneath the two eggs circling the frying pan and deposited them onto a couple of slightly burnt pieces of toast, this time with only minimal yolk spillage.

Lucas hated Mr. Sackhead. Had always hated him. The scarecrow had been haunting the north field of the family farm for as long as he could remember, and ever since he was a little kid the ragged figure had scared him. He still couldn't look the scarecrow in the face without a chill coursing through his belly.

His father knew this and poked fun at him whenever he got the chance. Lucas wouldn't be surprised if his dad had purposefully loosened the ropes that kept Mr. Sackhead on his post, just to make Lucas go out there and tie the scarecrow back up. His father loved his practical jokes.

Lucas's dad was gazing at him from over the edge of his newspaper, clearly expecting an answer. Lucas hesitated for only a second before stammering a quick, "S-sure, Dad. Whatever you say." Which was enough for the old man to return to his newspaper.

After breakfast was over and the dishes were scrubbed and blasted with hot water, Lucas threw on his chunky boots, permanently encrusted in mud, and went out into the crisp morning air. The sun hadn't fully risen just yet, so the shadows that pooled around the house were deep and purple. The heat of the day was still many hours away. It had rained heavily yesterday; the ground squelched underneath Lucas's feet as he rounded the old farmhouse and the north field came into view.

Long after harvest, the entire field was still covered in withered cornstalks, thick enough to hide anyone from view. The ground between the stalks was a muddy mess, covered by a cracked shell of dried earth that threatened to collapse under the slightest pressure. Even from here, Lucas could see the lopsided figure hanging from the solid wooden post in the distance, slightly higher than the stalks in his vantage point. The scarecrow was clothed in a wild mishmash of patterns and colors, stripes and polka dots meshing with bright plaids and solids. True to his name, his head was a lumpy potato sack stuffed full of odds and ends. Painted eyes decorated the old burlap. One of his fabric-clad arms dragged through the mud and his bulbous head leaned askew on one lumpy shoulder.

Sighing, Lucas trudged toward Mr. Sackhead, trying his best not to look directly at it. He was careful to push any stalks of corn out of his way long before they touched his face. They seemed unpleasant and slimy. Lucas sighed and swore to himself that this was the last time he'd string that awful thing back up. With the crops already harvested, there wasn't even any need for a scarecrow, but his father said it was tradition to keep him up all season long. Lucas suspected he just enjoyed creeping out his son.

Lucas glanced up and stopped dead in his tracks. High above the rows, the scarecrow's sack head was now leaned back. Lucas was positive that the head had been leaning on its shoulder, the scarecrow's painted eyes looking into the dirt at its feet. But now those cartoonish eyes were looking right at Lucas.

For a long time, Lucas just stood there. He considered turning around and going back to his father, putting his foot down for the first time in forever. He'd tell his old man to go hang his *own* scarecrow back up, if it was such a special tradition. Maybe his dad would finally take Lucas seriously for once! But he already knew that wouldn't happen.

Lucas continued his march through the rows of withered stalks, entering a small clearing where they had been crushed down into the mud. At the center of this circular space, he finally saw Mr. Sackhead up close. The bulbous burlap lump that stood for a head rested on skinny broomstick shoulders. Its mismatched clothes made Lucas's eyes water when he looked at them too long. He turned away, so as to prevent a migraine.

Reaching out, Lucas started pulling and pushing the scarecrow back onto its T-shaped post, holding his breath as he hastily tied its right arm back into place.

"C'mon, c'mon," Lucas muttered to himself. A cold sweat

broke out across his forehead. Carefully, he raised the grotesquely round and bloated head back into place and tied it down, trying his best not to look the thing in the eyes. Still, Lucas couldn't miss the awful face painted into the rough fabric. Aside from its giant eyes, the scarecrow had no other discernible features. But it only needed eyes to watch.

Lucas tied the final knot and stepped away to inspect his work. The scarecrow was back where it belonged and Lucas could continue ignoring it like he did most of the year. He still had lots of other chores to do today. Turning, he started along the same corn row that had brought him there, ignoring the low whispering of the stalks brushing against his sides. He was almost at the house when he got the strangest feeling, like someone was staring holes into him. Lucas reached the door and pulled it open, almost making it inside without giving in to the temptation to look behind him. But now that he stood safely on his doorstep, he couldn't resist.

That sense of safety immediately fell out from under him.

Mr. Sackhead's face had *turned* somehow, gazing over the long field toward the house—and Lucas. Which was impossible. Lucas had securely tied the scarecrow's head with its eyes forward, facing the *other* direction. He could still see the coils of strong rope looped over its lumpy forehead and the empty plane where its mouth should be.

Lucas swore he could feel those eyes on him. An old fear burned in his stomach, the same fear he'd had as a small child when he first saw the looming figure hanging from the post.

He shook it off quickly, though. "Didn't tie it tight enough, I guess," he muttered to himself. Then he closed the door and went inside. If his dad wanted to fix the old scarecrow again, he could do it himself.

In the field, a cold wind blew. If anyone had been watching, they might have said it looked for all the world like Mr. Sackhead was slowly writhing on its post, trying to break free.

CHAPTER FOUR
THE NEW HOME

Mary woke up from a fitful sleep, and for the longest time she had no idea where she was. She blew some of her curly black hair out of her face and rubbed her eyes. Sunlight angled in through the wide windows that spanned the front of their new house. Dust motes floated, caught in the beams. Mary sat up and threw off the sleeping bag haphazardly draped over her. Her parents were already up and puttering back and forth in their new kitchen, grabbing the ingredients they'd picked up at the grocery store as they started a big pancake breakfast. Her parents had made sure that they had enough kitchen implements in the car to at least make some flapjacks.

"How long have you guys been up?" Mary mumbled, rubbing the sleep from her eyes.

"Not very long," her father said. He stretched backward as if trying to relieve an ache. Presumably from sleeping on the hard wooden floor with nothing but a thin sleeping bag for comfort. "We wanted to let you sleep in. I know that was some drive."

"And today is going to be full of box hauling and unpacking!" her mom chimed in. "The moving van is due in an hour or so, so get ready." She didn't look up from the bowl of pancake batter she was cheerfully mixing.

Leaving them to their tasks, Mary opened a couple of boxes that had been brought in from the car and set haphazardly in the foyer. Pawing through them, she eventually found some clean clothes. Dressed for the day in some well-loved jeans and a T-shirt, it was finally time to explore her new home in earnest. Mary barely remembered the brief tour they'd gone on the previous night. She'd been so exhausted from the trip.

The sunlight filling the living room and kitchen only reached halfway up the staircase. Each step squeaked and groaned with protest as she ascended, the darkness of the upper landings drawing steadily closer. Thankfully, there was a light switch at the top of the stairs. As Mary flicked it, the upper floor of her new house came into view. She stood in a regular hallway, the walls covered with an old-fashioned paper design that seemed to curl and cross itself at every opportunity, all rendered in a faded robin's-egg blue. The heavy wooden doors were all firmly shut, which explained why the hall was so oppressively dark.

Mary made her way to each room and peered in. Unfortunately, the various bedrooms, guest rooms, and bathrooms weren't very exciting at all. For such an old house, she'd expected it to be a little spookier. As she looked in one dusty old space after another, Mary thought about everything she'd lost in the move. Her friends Sam and Gwen had promised that they'd keep in touch and visit eventually, after she'd had a chance to settle in. But who knew how long that'd take? Odds were that they had already moved on and were in the process of forgetting about her. That's how these things usually worked; it was easier that way.

Sighing, Mary tried her best to shake off those bad vibes like so much dust. It was important to have a positive outlook on things, she told herself. Finally, after a careful evaluation of all the rooms on offer, Mary decided that the bedroom at the end of the hall would be suitable. It was spacious and had a huge window on the far wall that she could already see herself curled up in front of, reading a good book.

Just as she'd resolved to claim the room over breakfast, she heard her mom approaching the staircase.

"Mary! Breakfast is ready!" Mom hollered, her voice echoing across the upper floor.

"Finally!" Mary said to herself. "I. Am. Starving." She left the bedroom and was making her way back toward the stairs when she heard it.

Just over her head there was a scratching sound. Mary paused mid-step and looked up, listening in case the noise repeated, but it didn't come again. Scanning the ceiling, she caught sight of a rectangular trapdoor that almost completely blended in with its surroundings. She remembered the cracked third-floor window she'd noticed last night when they'd first seen their new home. It was the perfect place for vermin to get in through.

"Mice . . ." she muttered. And wouldn't that just be perfect?

That trapdoor definitely led to an attic, and that'd be an ideal space for the little guys to hide. She shrugged and went downstairs to enjoy her first breakfast in her new house. Upstairs, unheard by anyone, the scratching started again.

Mary prodded her breakfast of pancakes, bacon, and orange juice. She sat with her parents, intently focused on pushing a wedge of pancake around her plate, slowly soaking up the syrup.

"So, Mary, what are your thoughts on our new abode?" her dad asked, spearing some bacon with his fork. "I heard you walking around up there while we slaved away making you breakfast. Does it meet your standards?"

"It's cool. I actually like how old this place is," Mary said, trying to keep her new positive outlook. In the fresh morning light, run-down *could* be interpreted as vintage. "It's got character."

"I'm glad to hear that," her mom said. "It's never easy to move to a new place, a new town. It's going to take some adjustment."

"When I was upstairs, though," Mary continued, "I thought I heard something. Like scratching in the ceiling. And I saw a little trapdoor in the hallway right around where I heard it. Maybe we have mice in the attic?"

Her dad paused in the middle of eating a pancake and pretended to choke in shock, his eyes bulging out of his head. Mary laughed like always.

"Honey, this place is old," he said. "It's seen a lot of history. If there are mice, then we'll deal with them. But let's not jump to conclusions."

"Well, as long as they stay away from the end of the hall and my new giant bedroom, then they can do whatever they like."

Mary's father and mother glanced at each other for a moment before turning back to their daughter. "Honey, uh, I'm sorry to say it, but that's going to be our bedroom," her dad said. "Your bedroom is the one on the right about halfway down the hall. We really need the space."

"What?!" she protested. "Why didn't you say any of that before I looked around? That bedroom is so small, and way crummier than the other one! And it's right by the trapdoor. I don't want to have to deal with mice all over my stuff! This is so unfair!"

"Honey, we're all dealing with these changes," her mom said, trying her best to soothe her. "But in the long run, everything will work out. I'm sure you'll get used to that room in no time at all.

And we're not even sure if there are any mice yet. You just heard a single noise."

"And if there *are* mice," her dad added, "I'll just give them the boot! This is our house now."

The first day in a new town and already things were going bad. Mary had been dragged all the way out here, away from her friends and everything she knew, and she didn't even have the luxury of deciding which room she got to sleep in. This was so unfair. If there were any mice in that attic who felt like they could intrude into her room, they had another thing coming.

CHAPTER FIVE

PEOPLE GO MISSING HERE

The corner of Piper Street stood deserted.

It was late at night. The rows of quiet cookie-cutter suburban homes were dark sentinels standing shoulder to shoulder, watching the wind blow dead November leaves along the sidewalks and empty street. The only light came from the third-floor window of a lonely house, right on the corner where Piper intersected with Browning Avenue. There, Byron Way was avoiding sleep and going over his notes yet again.

There'd been another disappearance this week, and this time it was someone he knew. One of Byron's few friends, Beverly, had gone missing while walking home after soccer practice. Usually, he would have been there to keep her company, but Byron had been forced to stay late after school for reading one of his horror novels in math class. Now Bev had disappeared. The rumor at school was that she'd run away from home, but Byron knew. Beacon Point had claimed another victim.

Byron didn't have very many friends at Beacon Point Middle School, and to a certain extent he understood. He preferred to read by himself during lunch periods. He was quiet, and his short, dull-brown hair and giant 70s-style glasses fit the look of a reclusive weirdo to a tee. Most people didn't bother looking past that and getting to know him.

But Beverly had. Despite being heavily into sports and not sharing very many interests with Byron, she had seen him eating lunch by himself one day and introduced herself. It wasn't long before they were eating together every day, Beverly trying to convince him to join her soccer team while he rambled on about the newest volume of whatever fantasy series he happened to be reading. And over time, a real friendship had grown.

Byron had spent his entire life in Beacon Point. He knew better than anyone that strange things happened here. Odd phenomena in the sky, bizarre animal sightings in the woods that bordered the town—some even claimed to have seen ghosts. People went missing every couple of years, and nothing ever got done about it.

Most adults in town seemed to take things in stride, as if a kid going missing now and then was normal. Byron had long ago started compiling all the evidence of strangeness he could find in a thick leather scrapbook his uncle had gifted him for his birthday, and now it was full of newspaper clippings, Polaroid photos, scrawled notes, and pencil sketches. Beverly had never really believed him, but she'd humored him when he talked about sightings of the Beacon Point bird monster at the abandoned factory or mutant deer in the woods. Byron didn't mind her skepticism. It was nice just to be heard.

Still, all the strange things that had happened in Beacon Point so far had happened to other people. They were stories Byron read about or listened to on Alan Graves's radio show. Byron had never thought people he knew might be in real danger.

Now Bev was missing. And with her disappearance came the confirmation that his town was rotten to its core. Even worse, it seemed like things were happening faster every day. More and more sightings, more missing people.

Byron was rereading an eyewitness account of a giant centipede sighting, trying his best not to think of Beverly out there somewhere in need of help, when he heard a noise outside. A clattering like animals in the garbage cans brought him to the small circular window that looked down on Piper Street. He was right. Even from here he could see fast-food packaging and old burgers scattered under a streetlight. A circular garbag-can lid had fallen and had just finished rolling to a stop. It fell on its side with a fresh clatter of noise.

Byron had almost turned back to his book when he noticed the figure standing in the street. They stood off from the glare of the streetlight, their features made indistinct by darkness.

Was someone really there, or were his tired eyes playing tricks on him? Byron gasped as a man stepped forward, his wide-brimmed hat and long coat suddenly visible in the harsh cone of light. Other than the approaching step, the figure stood motionless, with his head downcast. Byron's skin crawled with sudden fear. Something about the man's clothes struck him as exceptionally odd. They were archaic, as if the figure had emerged from a completely different time period.

Just as the stranger slowly raised his head toward the window, the streetlight went out and the scene was covered in darkness. Byron took a step back.

The light had died before he could make out any of the man's features, but he got the distinct impression that whoever the stranger was, he was still standing outside Byron's house, still looking at him through the thin sheet of glass that separated them.

Byron held his breath for what seemed like ages. Then, with a weak sputter, the streetlight flickered and came back on again.

The man was gone. Byron might have sworn the entire episode was a hallucination brought on by sleep deprivation, if not for the writing scrawled across the sidewalk where the figure had been standing.

Burned into pointed angles with eerie dark letters was a single word, spread wide so Byron could read it easily even from his third-story vantage point:

HELLO

"Weird . . ." Byron whispered.

Then he turned back to his desk—and screamed.

The man was standing in the corner of his room.

The stranger's wide hat draped his face in shadow, and his long, muddy coat almost scraped against the floor. Byron's desk lamp, the sole source of light in the bedroom, suddenly flickered out. Byron fell backward, paralyzed by fear, as the dark outline of the figure took first one step toward him, then another. Byron's AM/FM stereo—a birthday gift from his mother—lit up behind the stranger, casting his silhouette in pale green light. The air filled with radio static and snippets of different voices, each cut off almost before they could be heard.

"You . . . don't . . . know . . . what's . . . coming . . ." the radio squealed. "They . . . were . . . promised . . ."

Out in the hall, Byron heard frantic footsteps as his mom rushed to check on him. The radio turned off, throwing the room into darkness once more, and the static ceased. Then, just as suddenly as it had turned off, the desk lamp flickered back on.

Byron's room was empty, as if nothing had happened at all. He only had a moment to compose himself before his mom was bursting through the door.

"Byron!" she exclaimed. "Are you all right? I heard you scream! You just about gave me a heart attack in bed!"

"Sorry, Mom," Byron said, his voice still shaky. "I must have fallen asleep at my desk and had a nightmare. I'm fine now. Just going to go back to sleep—for real this time. Sorry for scaring you."

"Okay, baby, if you think you can manage it," she said. "If you need anything, please come ask, okay?" Then she slowly closed his bedroom door.

Byron heard her hesitant footsteps going back to her bedroom on the second floor.

He debated his next move. Something in Beacon Point had found him, maybe the same thing that had gotten Beverly. Involving his mom wasn't going to help. It would only put her at risk, too. He doubted he'd get to sleep tonight, but tomorrow he would have to start putting together a plan of action. This couldn't just be happening to him. This had sounded like a warning. It was time to reach out to some other kids before it was too late.

As Byron got into bed, his eyes focused on the ceiling, and he gasped in shock. Someone had written huge words overhead, obviously meant for him to see as he lay down to sleep. The letters warped even as he watched. They said:

SEE YOU SOON

CHAPTER SIX

BEHIND THE E—Z CONVENIENCE

Todd watched as the bottle he'd thrown toward the dumpster clonked off its chipped green side, spinning in midair for a moment before crashing to the asphalt in a heap of glass.

"Swing and a miss," he said to no one in particular.

He took another bite of his hoagie. He'd need to hurry if he was going to finish his lunch before reporting back to work at the store. Todd wasn't sure how many more warnings he could rack up before his job was in danger.

"Ah, they can wait," Todd muttered again to no one in particular. He'd been working weekend shifts at the E-Z Convenience for the last couple of months, and while the paychecks were nice, Todd was beginning to think that the sacrifice of his free time wasn't worth it. He was grateful for the position, even if it was just as a lowly clerk, but he was already reaching his limit. His only moment of quiet—away from rude customers and the overbearing gaze of his manager, Kenneth—was his snack break. During these breaks, Todd treated himself to a meatball sandwich from the warming station and a bottle of soda. Drinking from the glass bottles always made it taste better somehow.

It was just such a bottle that had exploded against the asphalt, however. He'd have to clean that up before the end of his shift.

Todd liked taking his breaks behind the store. There was a space by the service door that was far enough away from the dumpsters so the employees didn't have to catch a whiff of the smell. And it had an overhang that kept him from getting soaked when it stormed. It was one of the few times in his day when he could really be alone. His life had become so hectic lately. Struggles with school, his father making him take this job to provide his own "fun money," his general status as a pimply, friendless loser—all combined to make sure life was as difficult for him as possible.

Todd finished his sandwich. His mouth still full of meatball and bread, he balled up his sandwich wrapper and threw it to the dumpster. This time, the ball of tinfoil and grease-stained Saran Wrap passed neatly through the bin's open hatch.

"He shoots, he scores!" Todd shouted through a mouth full of food, spraying crumbs across the asphalt. He raised his arms in victory. He got to his feet and hopped down from the ledge he'd been sitting on, dusting crumbs off his jeans. He was about to make the short walk back into the store when he heard it.

Inside the heavy metal shell of the dumpster, something moved.

Glass bottles clinked together as whatever was inside shifted its weight, the sound echoing off the inner walls. There was a brief chattering noise—the call of some animal.

Raccoon, Todd thought immediately.

They often came out of the nearby woods to raid the convenience store's garbage. He'd seen them many times as he brought out the bags, their little reflective eyes caught in the light from the back door. Todd took a couple of tentative steps forward, craning his neck to try to see beyond the edge of the bin. But all he could see were the garbage-soaked edges of some cardboard boxes and a corner of black plastic.

He was about to give up and turn back, all the better to avoid having to tangle with a wild animal, when the noise came again. This time it was different. Like a long, low moan, but combined with that chattering noise he'd heard earlier. Suddenly, Todd was less sure that a raccoon was scavenging inside the bin.

He pictured an injured person, some poor victim of a mugging who'd been unceremoniously dumped into the trash. Maybe Todd could save somebody's life! He'd be a hero. He rushed to the edge of the dumpster without a second thought and peered over the edge, into the stinking depths.

"Hey! Hey!" Todd yelled. "Is someone there? Do you need help? Just say something and I'll run inside and call 911!"

He still couldn't see anything but old cardboard boxes and garbage bags. But to his shock, several muffled voices called back.

"Hey! Hey! Is someone there?"

It took Todd by such surprise that he stumbled backward and fell on his butt. From the dumpster, the same voices called again.

"Do you need help? Do you need help? Do you need help?"

Once more he heard the clinking of glass and the sounds of shifting garbage bags, but this time the entire dumpster started to rock in place. Something was coming out.

As it emerged, Todd could hardly process what he was seeing. The creature was long and red, with an exterior made of interlocking plates that caught the light. Todd scrambled back from his spot on the dirty asphalt, just taking in the massive, segmented length of it.

It was as wide as his torso and decorated on either side by countless piston legs. Massive feelers swung back and forth from the front of the creature as it touched down on the pavement, waving in his direction. Bits of wet garbage were slicked to the creature's bright red shell, the result of its unsavory nest, and the smell coming off it was sickening—like rotten fruit left in the sun.

As Todd watched, numerous horizontal slits split open along the creature's body. He felt faint as he realized that they were enormous toothy mouths.

"Need help?" the mouths chanted as one. "Need help? Need help?"

Todd sucked in a breath to scream.

As he did, the massive centipede rocketed toward him.

CHAPTER SEVEN
FACE AT THE WINDOW

Lucas was exhausted. He had spent his entire Saturday working away under his father's watchful gaze, and every joint in his body hurt. He'd even threatened to make him work Sunday, which was usually Lucas's day to himself. His temples throbbed, a headache surely on its way. The best thing to do now was to go to his room at the back of the house, maybe listen to some music, and get some sleep. The sun had long since set, and Lucas was more than ready to call it a day.

Lucas's room was sparse. He had a worn desk that they'd picked up from the side of the road one day, an old-fashioned steel bed frame with great brass knobs on all four corners, and a scratched-up nightstand. On the desk was Lucas's prized possession, an old boom box with a tape deck, and a small pile of albums on cassette tapes to go with it. The walls were plastered with torn band posters, most of them covered in Scotch tape to hide the rips. The only thing that was genuinely new was the mattress itself, which Lucas took the opportunity to fall onto without even turning the light off.

Monday was another school day, and as always, he was dreading it. Lucas's secondhand clothes and his oversized boots (his father's old pair) had quickly set him apart from his classmates. And he lived far from the suburban center of town, unlike all the other kids. It seemed like the harder he tried to fit in, the more he was held at arm's length. By now, he was past the point of caring, though. He didn't need friends to be happy, really.

And none of it mattered at the moment—not as much as sleep. Lucas sank into his mattress, finally feeling the aches and pains of the day begin to leave him. He was more than half asleep and pleasantly drifting when something clinked against the glass of his window, just to the right of his small bed. Lucas glanced, bleary-eyed, in that direction, but the light in his bedroom had rendered the window an opaque square of black.

It was easy to underestimate just how dark it got at night when you were away from other buildings, other houses. The shadows became overwhelming. Lucas doubted any of his classmates could understand, living as they did in the suburbs of Beacon Point. But darkness was something that he'd been intimately familiar with from a very young age. He didn't bother trying to peer out into that night until he'd turned off his bedside lamp.

There was nothing to see. Just the muddy earth of his backyard, which eventually gave way to the rows of withered stalks that swayed in the night breeze.

Lucas sighed, taking this chance to get ready for bed properly. He put on the baggy old Judas Priest shirt that he'd gotten from a thrift store in town, too big for regular wear but perfectly comfortable to sleep in. He kicked off his dirty, worn jeans and slid under the covers. He was almost asleep when the noise came again. A sharp sound, like a nail being scraped on glass. Barely there but loud as a gunshot in Lucas's dreaming mind. His eyes shot open and he rolled over to face the window, quickly stifling a scream.

He had the brief impression of a wide, horrible face peering at him from his window, already pulling back into the darkness. It had stretched from corner to corner of the sill, covering the glass in a horribly rough skin. The eyes were huge, dominating the entire face, leaving no room for a nose or a mouth.

For a moment there, Lucas was more scared than he'd ever

been in his life. Then he realized what had been pressed against his window. It was the face of Mr. Sackhead, probably blown off the scarecrow's body by a strong late-autumn wind. Somehow it had ended up here, caught against the house.

Lucas climbed out of bed and snapped his curtains shut. He was annoyed with himself for being so easily frightened. He lay back in bed and tried to get some sleep, but a nagging thought kept him awake. If he left the scarecrow as is, its sack head would keep blowing about in the breeze, and probably be lost for good. Then Lucas would never hear the end of it from his father. It had been Lucas's job to secure the stupid thing, after all.

No, it was better to correct things now while his father was asleep. Lucas tugged on his jeans and shirt and made his way through the quiet house, taking only a brief detour to the kitchen to grab the flashlight his father kept in the junk drawer. After tying up his boots, Lucas opened the back door. Quickly, before he could turn back from fear, he stomped out into the night.

First, he checked the window facing into his bedroom. His unmade bed looked very inviting, but the sack face was nowhere to be seen. The wind must have blown it away. He swore to himself that he would make this quick, just a look around for the scarecrow's head and then back to bed.

Making his way around the house along the familiar route, it wasn't long before Lucas found himself amid the dark corn rows. He stepped lightly, careful to avoid tripping over the deep furrows cut into the earth. But soon Lucas realized that something was very wrong. Panning his flashlight across the field brought no sign of Mr. Sackhead, only the T-shaped pole that usually supported the scarecrow. Lucas could only stare wide-eyed at the ropes dangling from the wooden struts, swaying slightly in the night breeze.

He glanced around, suddenly even more anxious to get back to the safety of his room. Forget the stupid scarecrow. He never should have come out here. Lucas started the walk back to the farmhouse, forcing himself not to run. If he didn't run, then obviously he wasn't scared of anything.

He tried not to think about how the rustling rows of cornstalks to his left and right could hide anyone, or any*thing*, from view. Tomorrow, once the sun was up, he and his father would find Mr. Sackhead, wherever he'd blown to. That would be that.

From a row over, Lucas swore he heard squelchy footsteps in the mud. He stopped, and the footsteps halted as well. Probably it was just his anxious brain playing tricks on him, but he didn't dare look through the stalks toward the source of the sounds. He started walking again, keeping the flashlight pointed directly in front of him as he followed the worn path back to the house. Every time Lucas paused, he was sure the footsteps stopped as well. And when he walked, he could hear them start again.

"Forget this," Lucas finally muttered to himself, and then broke into a run.

As he picked up speed, Lucas was sure he could hear his pursuer speeding up to match him. By the sound of it, the distance between them was shrinking. As his doorstep slid into sight between the cornstalks, Lucas's momentary relief quickly turned to panic. A gust of air brushed the back of his neck—warm as a breath. Lucas imagined a hand reaching for the collar of his shirt.

Now gasping for air, he pushed himself into a sprint. Lucas piled into the solid farmhouse door, crashing it open and then instantly slamming it shut behind him. His hand shaking, he hurriedly turned and locked the bolt. For a moment he only stood there with his back against the door, catching his breath—until a voice called from the darkened hall ahead.

"Lucas! What do you think you're doing up at this hour?!"

Just his father, awakened by the noise and slamming door.

"Sorry, Dad," Lucas huffed. "I thought I heard something and went to take a look. The scarecrow isn't on its post, and I thought I saw . . . Ah, never mind. It's fine."

"Well, we can deal with that tomorrow, okay? Just get to sleep!" his dad said.

"Yeah," Lucas agreed. "Night." He turned and quickly headed back to his room.

Was someone chasing me?

Now that he was safe inside, his earlier terror seemed ridiculous. But at the time, it had felt like there *was* a person out there in the field. Someone who wanted to do him harm. Lucas closed his bedroom door, and, after a moment, locked it as well. He turned back toward his bed and stopped dead in his tracks, his blood running cold.

Amid his tangled sheets and bedspread, someone had spread handfuls of moldy old straw.

Ep. 15
"Doppelgängers"
Partial transcript of the
BCON RADIO MYSTERY SHOW,
hosted by Alan Graves

Broadcast on Oct 7, 1993

**[Atmospheric eerie music plays,
wolves howling]**

Alan Graves: Hello, hello, hello again,
loyal listeners! Thank you for tuning
in to my humble program. I hope that
tonight's horrible history lesson will
be . . . fulfilling for you. There's always a
new terror tale to tell in Beacon Point.

Today I want to ramble on about one
of the more persistent legends from
this particular neck of the woods, the
mysterious doppelgänger. As late as

the early 70s, there have been sporadic sightings of so-called doppelgängers, or face-thieves, in and around Beacon Point. One such case was the disappearance of Anthony Cryer in 1974. Anthony was a teacher at the local elementary school at the time and, on weekends, he loved nothing more than to go hiking along one of the many trails that snake through our woods. But on one of these lonely hikes, Anthony went missing. It wasn't until Monday morning when he didn't show up for class that the local authorities were alerted and a manhunt began.

And in a rare turn for Beacon Point disappearances, he was actually found—a little scratched up, a little dehydrated, but with no real lasting damage . . . or so it seemed.

Over the next couple of weeks, and then months, Anthony's students noticed a change in their beloved teacher. Whereas before he was compassionate and kind, an endlessly patient figure for the children to look up to, the Anthony who came back from the woods was cold and strange. A couple of students even told their parents in no uncertain terms that the thing that was teaching their class was no longer human.

Then, one day, Anthony walked out of his class with all his students marching behind him. He didn't speak a single word to another soul or send home any permission slips for this little field trip. Anthony and his entire fifth-grade class disappeared into the nearby woods, and despite numerous search parties, none of them were ever seen again. Some say that the thing that came back from that initial doomed hiking trip wasn't Anthony at all but a face-thief. It took over his life for a short period of time, only to lead more victims into the waiting forest. These creatures are said to be able to perfectly mimic a human being of their choosing, often fixating on one victim. There have been many cases in Beacon Point where suddenly, family members turned on their own, claiming their loved ones were impostors!

Once the creature is found out, it will often reveal its monstrous true form.

When that happens, according to myths and certain accounts, the creature will attempt to kill anyone who saw it out of disguise before moving on to find a new host to imitate. So . . . is the story of the doppelgänger just rampant paranoia, or is there actually a creature in Beacon Point that can perfectly imitate a friend, a loved one, maybe even someone YOU know? Maybe it's best to keep a close eye on those around you. You never know, right?

[End of broadcast]

CHAPTER EIGHT
CONSPIRACIES OVER LUNCH

Mary had only just started settling into her new house when her first day of school arrived. She hadn't even gotten the chance to explore Beacon Point yet, aside from her quick glances from a speeding car. The weekend had been a slog of unpacking, and now the time had come to start attending classes at Beacon Point Middle School.

Her morning homeroom class and English went by in a dull blur. Mary felt a dim embarrassment to be attending her first class a couple of months later than all the other students. She missed her old friends and teachers. She missed her old routine, no matter how much it had frustrated her at the time. Mary tried her best to push these feelings aside. It wasn't her fault that she'd been uprooted and dragged here against her will, but there was no point in being sad about things she had no hope of changing.

She realized she'd been lost in thought only when her new English teacher, Ms. Simmons, tapped her on the shoulder.

"I'm so sorry, Mary. It's your first day of class, and we're already boring you, I see."

"Not at all, Ms. Simmons," Mary grumbled through gritted teeth.

"Well then, how about we do a little exercise to help you meet your new classmates?" Ms. Simmons said smugly.

Soon, Mary was standing in front of the class and being forced to talk about herself. As she rambled on about her favorite food (pierogies) and her favorite color (fuchsia), she looked out over the sea of blank faces. Mary caught a flicker of movement out of the corner of her eye. For a moment she was sure that a looming figure, clad in a long coat and a wide hat, stood by the door to the hall.

"I . . . um . . ." Mary managed to say while the class looked on with concern. It was only after a moment that she realized what she'd mistaken for a figure was really just old clothes draped on a coatrack. Behind her, Ms. Simmons sighed.

"That'll be all, Ms. Hargrove. Very illuminating."

Mary rushed to her seat, her cheeks red with embarrassment. She waited out the rest of class with her head on her desk.

When lunchtime finally came, it was nothing short of a relief. Mary grabbed her brown paper bag and joined the crowds of kids making their way to the back of the school. While there was a cafeteria inside, it was already pretty full. Instead of trying to find a seat, Mary made her way outside. The back of the school had a small area set aside for eating, little more than a grassy patch studded with four weathered old picnic tables. They were set up around a thick old oak tree, its bare branches stretching toward the sky like skeletal fingers.

Mary had only just unpacked her lunch—a peanut butter and honey sandwich, apple slices, and milk—when she was startled by someone plopping down in the seat across from her. It was a tall, thin boy with a shaggy blond mullet. He wore a military-green button-up that matched his eyes, over an inscrutable T-shirt for a band she'd never heard of. A couple of small holes had torn just under the collar, and when he saw that Mary had noticed them, he pulled his coat tighter.

"Can I sit here?" he asked, eyeing her warily. "There's nowhere else right now."

"Sure, go for it," Mary responded evenly. "Be my guest."

The boy offered his hand. "I'm Lucas. Lucas Weaver."

"Mary Hargrove." She took his large hand in her own smaller one, and he gave it two big shakes. Lucas bit into the sandwich he'd brought with him, something meaty stuck between two huge hunks of bread.

"Now we know each other!" Lucas said ecstatically around a mouthful of food, cracking a lopsided grin. "I don't recognize you. You new? You must be new." He swallowed and immediately took a big swig of water.

"It's that obvious, huh? Yeah, you called it. Me and my parents just pulled into town a couple days ago. I've barely looked around yet. Doing the helpful daughter thing, you know? Unpacking, definitely not resentful about moving here."

To Mary's relief, Lucas chuckled. "Well, let me be the very first person to welcome you to Beacon Point. I am the first person, right?" Lucas searched dramatically for anyone else who might have beaten him to the punch, holding his hand flat over his eyes.

Now it was Mary who laughed. This guy was an absolute weirdo, but she found herself warming to him. "The first kid, anyway. Relax!"

"I live on my dad's farm out on the edge of town," Lucas said. "So I know a bit about the dutiful kid routine. I help him keep everything running smoothly when I'm not at school. It's basically like it's *my* farm and I just let him live there. Got the full run of the place."

Mary put on an impressed face. "I don't doubt it at all. But I can beat that. We moved into the spooky place on Aickmen Lane. It's really run-down, but my parents want to make a big deal out of fixing it up and making it really nice."

Mary took a couple more bites of her sandwich but was already *way* behind Lucas and his apparently voracious appetite. She found she wasn't that hungry anyway. She was happy to sit back and let Lucas talk.

"The big place on Aickmen? Wow, I never thought anybody would move in there. I've lived in Beacon Point my entire life and that house has always, always been empty. There's a ton of rumors about it, y'know? People used to say it was haunted."

Mary stifled a laugh and said, "Haunted? Really? It might look like it, but there's no such thing as haunted houses or . . ." But she trailed off as she saw the serious expression on Lucas's face.

"I didn't used to believe in that sort of thing myself, but . . ." Lucas sighed. "Lately, I . . . I'm not so sure. Things on the farm have been . . . a little strange."

Before Mary had a chance to ask him just how strange, he forged on.

"But the Aickmen place . . . well, there used to be rumors of strange lights and noises there. People would claim to see movement in the windows late at night, even though everyone knew it had been deserted for years. A kid I knew once said he actually saw *monsters* in your backyard."

Lucas laughed at this. Mary chuckled along, too, but she wasn't so sure she found it funny. She kept hearing the scratching sounds from the attic replaying in her head, and Lucas's laughter rang hollow.

"Honestly," Lucas said, "I don't know any place in Beacon Point that doesn't have some scary rumor floating around about it. If you listen to some of the folks around here, you'd think the entire town is cursed. It *can* be a really odd place." Lucas gave her a worried look, as if he wanted to tell her something important but didn't know how.

Mary regarded this haunted-looking boy, her sandwich long forgotten. Despite his feigned skepticism, something had clearly spooked him. What was up with this town?

"What exactly do you mean by your farm being strange?" she ventured.

But before Lucas could answer, a shadow fell over the table.

"This town is *full* of monsters."

A new person slid into the seat to Mary's left.

Whereas Lucas was tall and lanky, this new boy was small. He wore a long coat that almost swallowed him up, and his face was dominated by a big pair of thick black-rimmed glasses.

"I heard you talking about Beacon Point, and I *distinctly* heard the word *strange* as well. I'm Byron Way. Pleased to meet you. Hello, Lucas."

"Byron . . ." Lucas said tightly.

Mary was speechless for a second, before finally finding her voice.

"Hello. Byron? Nice to meet you, too. Please, uh, sit with us. Be my guest."

If Byron noticed the tension, he chose to ignore it. "You're new, right?" he asked. "Sorry to hear that. No one wants to find out they just moved into a town full of paranormal creatures and ghosts and whatnot."

Mary wasn't sure how to even engage with this . . . person who had joined their conversation. She decided on a noncommittal "Oh, really?"

For his part, Lucas simply rolled his eyes and looked away. Mary guessed that Byron was well-known at Beacon Point Middle.

"Really," the boy said. "For a long time, it wasn't so bad. You'd hear some strange stories, sure, but they never hit close to home. Lately, though, kids have been going missing. My friend Beverly disappeared a few days ago." Byron's energy momentarily left him.

"Wait," Lucas said. "Beverly, that sporty girl? I'm so sorry. Does anyone know what happened?"

"Not officially," Byron said, lowering his voice. "But *I* know. The monsters got her."

He seemed as if he was worried about people listening in on their conversation. He was silent for a moment before continuing.

"One of them appeared in my room the other night." Byron raised his eyebrows, glancing from Lucas to Mary and back again, trying to gauge their reactions. When neither responded right away, he sighed in disappointment.

"You don't believe me," he said. "I knew no one would believe me yet. But just wait, things are only going to get scarier around here."

He grabbed the remains of his lunch and stood.

"I'll be around if you want to reach out. And in the meantime, I'd be careful if I were you. This place has a long, *long* history of monster sightings. When things get bad, it's best that we stick together."

And with that, Byron stalked away.

Mary and Lucas looked at each other, unsure of what had just happened. Before they could say anything, however, the bell went off, signifying the end of lunch.

"Well, that was Byron," Lucas said, a little sheepishly. "He's always like that. You'll get used to it. Or not."

Lucas stood and gathered his things to go. As he turned to look at Mary, he ran a hand through his mullet. "I-it really was nice to meet you. Let's have another lunch filled with paranoid monster conspiracies very soon."

Mary laughed. "Likewise. This was . . . uh . . . interesting."

And soon Mary was in her first math class, busy just trying not to be left behind. By the time the school day finished, she'd all but forgotten about the strange kid and his ominous warnings.

Ep. 22

"Messages from the Stranger" Partial transcript of the BCON RADIO MYSTERY SHOW, hosted by Alan Graves

Broadcast on Dec 9, 1993

[Ominous music plays, theremin music swells]

Alan Graves: Hey there, eager listeners, boys and ghouls, denizens of our quiet little commune, nestled so perfectly in the arms of the wild woodlands. If you've listened to even one episode of the BCON RADIO MYSTERY SHOW, then you already know that our town is bursting with monsters and ghosts, myths and legends, mysteries and terrors. Personally, I wouldn't have it any other way. It's just so interesting, wouldn't you agree? But today, I want to speak to you about one of the more charismatic creeps that supposedly calls this patch of land home: the Beacon Point Stranger. Now, there are lots of stories about ominous figures lurking on the periphery of normal society. The black-eyed children seen in Texas and Oregon, the famous men in black associated with many UFO sightings. But the Stranger is a little different from these unsavory characters.

The Stranger is a tall, imposing character, always seen wearing his trademark long black coat and wide-brimmed hat. His face is almost always in shadow, and some say that it's so ghastly to witness that anyone who sees it loses their mind. I'd say that's mighty kind of him, keeping a face like that hidden.

The Stranger has been sighted off and on in Beacon Point for many, many years. But if you believe the stories—and dear listener, I know that you do—he started out as a kindly librarian who lived right here in Beacon Point. Back in the late 1800s, he was one of the early settlers who helped start this town, turning it into the gem that it is today. Going by the name Crawford Foley, he was an imposing figure at just over six feet tall. Walking the town square in his intimidating coat and hat, you'd forgive the other denizens of Beacon Point if they crossed the street when they saw him coming.

That said, they were wrong to do it, for by all accounts Crawford was one of the kindest people you could ever meet. He set about making the Beacon Point Library into a real treasure trove of information, something the town could be proud of. But Crawford was the nervous sort; he kept to himself. It wasn't long before rumors started being whispered about him, that he'd uncovered some very odd books and was communing with ancient forces that lurked beneath the town.

Perhaps the whispers started to get to him. Or perhaps there was some truth to the stories. Because by all accounts, Crawford changed. His demeanor became stranger, meaner. What few friendships he'd made since establishing himself in the new town fell away.

This all came to a head one night when a fire broke out in the library. No one knows what started the blaze, but with all those books as fuel, it didn't take long for the entire building to get caught up. Crawford was frantic. Before anyone could stop him, he ran into the burning building, screaming about something precious in his basement workshop. By the time the fire department, such as it was at the time, arrived to put out the now roaring inferno, there was nothing anyone could do. The building burned long into the night. By morning it was nothing but singed beams and wet ash and piles of charred books.

The next day, fire officials uncovered the basement room that Crawford used as a workshop, expecting the worst. But there was nothing to find. No body, no nothing. Crawford was gone, never to be seen again.

There were rumors about other things uncovered in the basement ruins, however. Eerie books and objects. Jars of mysterious chemicals and odd powders. But this is all unconfirmed, of course.

It wasn't until a few years later that people started seeing Crawford. Or at least the thing that was now wearing his clothes. The Stranger was often spotted walking through town in the middle of the night. Occasionally, witnesses would claim they'd seen him lurking outside people's homes, or watching through bedroom windows in the early morning. Then came the disappearances. Folks who'd been the source of all those whispers about Crawford when he was alive. Then just anyone who was unlucky enough to see him wandering the town at night. One of the most interesting details about the disappearances was that the Stranger would always leave messages. Incoherent and ominous missives were etched into the homes of those taken, taunting their loved ones. It was as if the words had been burned into the wood.

Crawford Foley is rarely seen these days, but watch out for his warnings, his scrawled portents of doom. If you see one,

it may mean that the Stranger is coming
for you next.

Until next time, I'm Alan Graves, the only
radio host giving you local lessons in
supernatural history.

[Maniacal laughter SFX, wind blowing SFX]

[End of broadcast]

CHAPTER NINE
MIDNIGHT VISITOR

Lucas lay in bed, his eyes following the cracks that splayed across his bedroom ceiling.

It was a bright night, as rural nights went. The sky was empty of clouds and a full moon shone through the window, illuminating the foot of his bed. The shadow of an old tree out in the yard cast shadowy fingers across his room.

As much as he wanted to get some sleep before school tomorrow, Lucas knew he couldn't. He was expecting a visitor. Someone had been trespassing on the farm, and this time, he was determined to catch him.

His dad didn't believe him. As far as he was concerned, Lucas was a little kid, and kids made up stories all the time. When Lucas had told him about being followed through the cornstalks the other night, his dad had actually scoffed. He said Lucas was too easily spooked.

But over the past couple of nights, the trespasser had returned over and over again.

Lucas had found footprints in the mud outside his window. Peering through it last night, he was sure he'd caught a glimpse of someone darting out of sight. But whenever he tried to catch this mysterious person, he was always just a little bit too late.

Mr. Sackhead still hadn't turned up, either. Lucas was sure that it was part of this strange campaign against him. Probably some local bullies who had decided the poor farm boy was a perfect punching bag for the remainder of the school year. He could picture the scarecrow now, defaced and propped up in some kid's closet. Truth be told, Mr. Sackhead's disappearance was the only part of this that Lucas was fine with. As far as he was concerned, the trespassers could keep the ugly old thing.

Though there *was* the matter of his father.

His dad thought that Lucas had hidden the scarecrow as some petty act of revenge. The morning after its disappearance, he gave Lucas a stern talking-to. Lucas had pleaded that he had no idea where Mr. Sackhead was—that he'd been out the previous night *searching* for the creepy old thing. But his dad simply stressed that he had better find it and get it back up on its post before the week was out, or the punishment would be severe.

Lucas wouldn't put it past his old man to do something drastic. Maybe he'd scrap the old car Lucas had been working on, or lock him in his room for the remaining weekends of the year.

Lucas sighed. While his dad was right about the grudge he had for the scarecrow, he didn't understand just how much the wretched thing disgusted and scared him. Lucas closed his eyes for a moment. He could still picture its awful sackcloth face stretched across his window, the painted eyes seeming to stare right at him.

Any chance he had of falling asleep evaporated beneath the memory of that stare.

Opening his eyes, Lucas caught a flash of movement outside. The beam of moonlight had been occluded, casting the room in darkness. Lucas leapt out of bed, but by the time he was up, the shadow had already disappeared.

Again he was a moment too late to see who was out there! But it had to be the same person. This was his chance to catch the jerk before they slipped away!

Lucas threw back his covers and tugged on the boots he'd kept by his bed, waiting for this very moment. He was still fully dressed from the day before. He wouldn't be caught off guard. Throwing on a thick coat and warm hat, he hurried down the hall toward the back door. Memories of the last night he'd gone out alone played across his mind. This might be his last shot at finding Mr. Sackhead—and the trespasser.

Outside, the fields were bathed in pale moonlight, in stark contrast to the darkness of the previous night. Lucas hurried along the house to his window, but no one was there. He searched around desperately. Had he been too slow yet again? But no—there! Lucas caught another flash of movement from the corner of his eye. There was someone moving in the rows!

A figure was moving through the stalks, heading toward the

nearby woods. Whoever it was, they were very tall and lanky, and much quicker than he'd expect from someone that size. They took wide, confident strides.

But there was something odd about the way they walked. Their arms hung loose at their sides, and Lucas couldn't shake the strange impression of bonelessness. After only a moment's hesitation, Lucas broke into a run.

"There's no way you're getting away from me again," he muttered under his breath. "Not this time."

Lucas dashed through the cornstalks, pushing them away from his face as he chased the trespasser.

It was strange. Whereas Lucas was running as fast as he could, the figure seemed to be hurrying. And though he was desperate to catch up to the stranger before they reached the cover of the surrounding trees, he was only just keeping up. Eventually, Lucas had to stop and catch his breath. He was bent over, clasping his knees with his hands, when he saw that the figure had also stopped.

Lucas was only yards away, but with the figure's back turned, it was impossible to make out any details. The light of the full moon turned them into a raggedy silhouette, all sharp edges of hanging cloth and long limbs.

"Hey!" Lucas shouted. "What do you think you're doing on my property? I know it's been you coming around here. What are you trying to prove by taking our stuff and knocking on windows in the middle of the—"

But he stopped when the figure turned abruptly to face him.

Lucas gasped. He took a step backward, nearly falling over in his fright. Even from this distance he could see the figure's face. It was a face that he'd have recognized anywhere.

Mr. Sackhead.

It only took Lucas a moment to get the sudden spike of fear under control. It was clear what had happened. Whoever stole the scarecrow was simply wearing its face as a mask, to scare him and to conceal their identity.

Still, seeing the intruder this close, it was clear from their height that this wasn't a middle-school student.

"Ha, ha, very funny," Lucas said nervously. "Why don't you get out of here before I call the police? My dad will be out here any second with his shotgun. Trust me, you don't want to mess with him."

The figure in the scarecrow mask stood motionless. If Lucas hadn't known any better, he might have thought it really was Mr. Sackhead.

Lucas started backing away in the direction of the house, being careful not to look away from the stranger. But whoever they were, they didn't move a muscle.

"I'm serious," he said again. "You better go right now. I know you don't want the cops—" Lucas stumbled, his feet tangling up in a knot of corn husks behind him, and he only glanced away from the scarecrow for a second, but when he looked back up, its sackcloth mask was inches from his nose.

Lucas screamed and fell backward, scrambling away from the awful figure. The scarecrow took a long step toward him, swaying as it moved. Its painted face was fixed on him, the burlap sagging back and forth on its shoulders.

Lucas leapt to his feet and ran for his house as fast as he could. Behind him, the scarecrow loomed, easily keeping pace. Lucas glanced back over his shoulder and was shocked to see that Mr. Sackhead was slowly disintegrating as it moved, the thick cornstalks tearing at its frame. In what felt like slow motion, Lucas watched the masked head topple left and right, squirming with odd shapes below its surface. Then it fell right off the figure's shoulders.

Lucas paused in shock as the headless body behind him tottered in place, before collapsing into a pile of brightly patterned cloth.

For a moment, the moonlit farm was silent. Then he noticed faint movements. All at once, a mass of beetles, cockroaches, and maggots poured out of the empty clothes, accompanied by a swarm of screeching rats. Lucas stifled another scream, backing away from the creeping, crawling animals. His gaze fell on the severed sack head.

For a moment, it lay motionless on its side, its painted eyes looking right in his direction. Then long, spidery limbs erupted from the burlap, easily piercing the fabric. The legs pressed into the earth, raising the mask upright.

Mr. Sackhead's face seemed to regard Lucas for a horrible beat, before it turned and scuttled away with alarming speed. He watched it disappear into the corn, its passage marked only by the moving stalks. The bugs and rodents also fled into the night, following the head to the forest's edge.

Before long, Lucas was alone in his father's field.

CHAPTER TEN
HOME BEFORE DARK

As long as the streetlights weren't lit yet, it didn't count as staying out after dark. At least that's what Jeremy reasoned as he furiously pedaled, trying not to lose his balance as he sped down through Beacon Point's downtown on his beat-up old bike.

He knew he was in for a lecture, but if he could get home before his mom did, he might still be okay. And it wasn't his fault, really. He'd been having such a good time playing video games with his friend Rebecca that the setting sun just sort of snuck up on them. It was already sinking below the horizon when he finally realized what time it was. Then the warning his mother had given him about staying out after dark hit him in a flash. Jeremy had scrambled out with little more than a stammered apology.

While he'd been lost in the rhythm of his feet pumping the pedals, the sky had faded from orange to red and finally to a deep purple. The color reminded Jeremy of a bruise he'd once suffered after a particularly nasty fall from his bike.

It was spooky how empty the streets of Beacon Point became as soon as the sun went down, like there was an unofficial curfew that everyone silently respected, even the adults. Most families must have gone inside to enjoy their dinners and get some sleep, Jeremy thought. He wished he were among them, already safe and warm at home, not rushing through the cold darkness, anticipating a lecture.

But even as he noted the deserted streets, he saw someone.

Way down at the end of the block, a lone man stood under one of the streetlights now blinking awake, just a blurry figure pinned under the sharp cone of light. He wore a wide-brimmed hat and a long coat that brushed his shins, but harsh shadows obscured his face of any other identifying details.

In that moment of distraction, Jeremy's bike must have hit something in the road. Before he knew what was happening, his front tire veered into a slide and he toppled to the rough asphalt with a thud.

The next few moments were a blur. Jeremy had the wind knocked out of him, and it took some work regaining his senses. But after a bit, he sat up, dazed.

The road was fully dark now, lit only in small circles cast from rows of streetlights.

The man he had seen was gone.

With a groan, Jeremy pulled his bike up from its horizontal position on the ground, inspecting himself for cuts or bruises. Then something caught his eye. On the redbrick wall in front of him, someone had scrawled a phrase in wide black letters.

Jeremy paused and stared at the graffiti. Peering closer, he saw that the letters weren't painted on the brick. Rather, it looked as if they'd been *burned* into the wall. He shuddered. It almost felt like the message had been written for him.

Looking around and seeing nothing but empty streets, Jeremy shrugged it off and got back on his bike. He could worry about the phantom graffiti when he was safely home. It was only getting darker. He set off again, his legs slowly pedaling faster and faster, gathering speed, the rhythmic clicking of the bike chain the only sound echoing through the empty block.

Jeremy kicked himself for forgetting his bike lamp, but he wasn't supposed to have needed it. He was supposed to be home.

Suddenly, he sucked in a ragged breath. The man in the hat was back, this time standing in the middle of the upcoming intersection. He was blurry with distance but still all too real.

Jeremy almost crashed his bike for the second time that night as a jolt of panic struck him. He glanced away from the figure as he straightened his wheel, and when he looked back, the man had disappeared again.

That . . . that wasn't possible. People didn't move that fast.

For the first time, Jeremy wondered just how much trouble he might be in.

He was almost home now, tearing down the middle of the street. But as he passed the local butcher shop, now shuttered for the night, Jeremy saw more graffiti burned into the wall. He only caught a glimpse as he sped by, but the writing was big and clear.

His heart pounding, Jeremy spared a quick glance over his shoulder. There was the eerie figure, standing still in the street about twenty feet back. Jeremy made a sudden left turn, obscuring the man behind a corner barbershop. Before long, the small downtown business area had given way to the manicured lawns and gardens of suburbia. Whatever was happening, if he made it home, he'd be safe. His mom would certainly be back by now. Jeremy didn't care if he got in trouble anymore. He'd take a thousand lectures if it meant not seeing that strange figure again.

But then another piece of graffiti slid into view, written in the same spidery scrawl as the other two messages. Only this time the message spanned the entire width of the road:

RIGHT BEHIND YOU

Jeremy forced back tears. He could still make it. He was only a street away from his house. In moments he'd be riding his bike up the driveway and throwing it to the lawn as he sprinted for the front door, his house key already clenched between his sweaty fingers. He could almost feel his palm on the doorknob, hear the satisfying slam of the door closing behind him.

But all these visions were crushed as his house came into view, the windows dark. His mother wasn't home yet.

And worse, the man in the wide-brimmed hat stood on his porch, waving from Jeremy's front door. He was closer than ever before, and taller than Jeremy would have thought possible. But his face was still obscured in shadow. The man spread his arms in greeting and stepped into the light.

The last thing Jeremy saw was the wide, moonlike face underneath that hat. The man's skin was pale and featureless, all except for his long and horrible mouth, which spread from one side of his head to the other. He smiled at Jeremy, his rotten teeth carved into a terrible rictus grin.

CHAPTER ELEVEN
THE ATTIC

Mary was startled awake by the scratching sound.

Again.

It wasn't the first time. She'd been hearing it ever since she'd started sleeping in her new room, though only recently had it become loud enough to wake her.

"Mice," she muttered to herself with utter scorn. Of course she'd been right. They had pests. And her parents had under-estimated how annoying they could be.

"Mice and other household pests are common," her dad had said. "But we'll deal with them if they pop up again."

Yet here it was, nearly a week later, and not a single extermi-nator had been called. Reminding herself that mice didn't usually bite, Mary drifted off to sleep again. But it wasn't long before the scratching started again, and this time it didn't let up. The sound was faint but annoying, like a fingernail worrying at the same spot over and over.

When morning finally arrived, Mary decided she was fed up.

At the breakfast table, she pushed her cereal around the bowl and stared sullenly ahead.

"Dad, remember that scratching sound I told you about?"

"Of course I do," her dad said, munching thoughtfully on his bacon. "Are you hearing it again?"

"Yes! And it's very loud. Plus, the thought of those mice up there is grossing me out! Can you please, *please* go check the attic?"

"And disturb your new friends?" he joked, taking a sip of orange juice. "Why would I ever do that?"

"Dad, please!" Mary dropped her spoon into her bowl, lightly spraying the table.

"Okay, okay!" he said. "I'm on it right now. Don't worry." And with that, Mary's dad pushed his chair away from the table.

Dad explored a broom closet in the front hall and found a long wooden stick with a thin hook on the end. But despite how imposing it looked, it was just used to pull down the old-fashioned unfolding staircase from the hallway ceiling.

To Mary, the stairs leading up to the attic looked like a long tongue stretching into a gaping mouth. As her dad climbed into the attic, she watched his flashlight beam bouncing around, and held her breath for what he might find.

Alone in the hallway, Mary thought about what Lucas and Byron had said about Beacon Point—specifically her house. Waiting for her father to emerge from the darkness above, it was all too easy to believe the place could be haunted. She was just readying herself to follow her father when suddenly he was climbing back down into the light.

"Nothing up there but cobwebs and dusty old furniture," he said. "Must have been left behind by the previous owners, whoever they were."

But Mary knew that something was up there. She hadn't just imagined the scratching!

Her dad promised to look into an exterminator, but Mary suspected that would take a long time. Both of her parents were so stressed about the unpacking, she knew she couldn't count on their full attention anytime soon.

The next night, the noises were the worst they'd been so far. They were so loud that her parents definitely should've heard them from their room at the end of the hall. The scratching hadn't disappeared. It had grown in its insistence and ferocity, and was now joined by a soft pacing, as if someone was walking incessantly back and forth over her head. Whatever was living in the attic was no mere household pest. Mary needed to stop it from getting out. She imagined some night where the noises paused, only to begin again outside her room. She imagined her doorknob slowly starting to turn . . .

The next day, Mary tried to appeal to her mother for help.

"Mom, I know Dad already checked out the attic, but I'm still hearing things. It's not just mice or rats up there! I'm sure of it!"

"And what do these non-mice sound like, exactly?" her mother replied calmly, putting down the novel she'd been reading.

"It's like scratching, and then footsteps! It goes on all night!"

"Your father and I haven't heard anything, and that certainly sounds like something that would have woken us. You know he's a light sleeper."

"I know, but it's loud enough that I can't sleep!"

"It's probably just the house settling. Or the pipes! Old houses like this have their own noises. We just have to get used to them. Give it time." With that, Mary's mom returned her attention to her book.

That night, Mary waited in bed and pretended to sleep. It wasn't long before the scratching commenced again.

Was her house actually haunted? Mary was afraid, but she couldn't listen to this forever. She threw the covers back and grabbed both the flashlight and red Swiss Army knife that she'd hidden under her pillow. She crept out of her bedroom, into the dark and empty hall. As she approached the trapdoor in the ceiling, the noises suddenly stopped. The shift from deafeningly loud to deathly quiet was jarring.

As Mary brought her flashlight up, she was shocked to see that someone had beaten her here. The attic hatch was wide open, and someone had extended the ladder. Small, dusty footprints led down the ancient wooden stairs to the hallway she'd just been walking. Whatever had been scratching on her ceiling at night was no longer content to stay in the attic. It had gotten into the rest of the house.

Even as this thought occurred to her, Mary was startled by the sound of footsteps on the floor below her.

They were headed up, slowly ascending the stairs.

A shiver of panic ran through Mary. As quietly as possible, she made her way back to her room and pulled the door closed until it clicked. Mary fumblingly switched off her flashlight, submerging the room in darkness.

She pressed her ear to the rough wood of the heavy door, listening for approaching noises. She didn't have to wait long.

The small tapping steps had reached the top of the stairs, and now made their way down the hall. They moved closer and closer before finally stopping right in front of her door. There was a dreadful beat of pure silence. The only sounds Mary could hear were her heart beating and her own quiet, shallow breaths. Then the scratching resumed again.

This time, it wasn't separated by rafters and plaster and a dusty old attic. The sound was right in front of her; her bedroom door was the only barrier she had.

Long, ragged nails scraped down the wood, inches from her ear.

Then, abruptly, the footsteps retreated. After a few agonizing moments, all was silent again.

Mary breathed in and out in an attempt to slow her thumping heart. When she finally felt calm enough, she cracked open the door—enough to turn on her flashlight and catch the edge of the attic stairs.

She was just in time to see the trapdoor slide back into place.

Mary needed to figure out what was living in her new attic, and she needed to do it *now*. Once she knew, she'd find Byron and Lucas at school and they could figure out a plan to get rid of it. Suddenly, the idea of this town being infested with monsters didn't seem so wild.

She trudged down the stairs the next morning, managing to mumble out a fatigued *good morning*. As she took a seat at the table, her parents commented on the bags under her eyes.

"I'm fine," Mary lied. "I just think I might be getting sick is all."

"You are looking a little under the weather," her mom said carefully. "We have to pick up a few things for the house, but maybe it's best if you stay home and get some rest."

Faking a low cough into her hand, Mary responded with, "Whatever you think is best."

But as soon as she heard her parents close and lock the front door, Mary grabbed a flashlight and ran up the stairs. She stood for a moment beneath the ominous attic hatch, which looked as if it had never been disturbed.

Grabbing the hooked stick from where Dad had left it, she reached up and slowly, carefully pulled the staircase down. Mary hesitated, terror rooting her in place. The hole to the attic was like a black void. But she had to know what she was sharing her new home with.

Trembling a little, she slowly climbed the attic steps. She told herself she would just take a quick look, always keeping the open hatch in sight, ready to run at the first sign of danger.

But the attic was mostly empty—like her dad had said. There was only an ancient-looking chest of drawers, the rusty remnants of a metal bed frame, and a couple of moldy boxes. She almost gave up and headed back downstairs right then. Maybe whatever was making the noise was a ghost, and only appeared at night. She'd started to turn back to the attic hatch when she noticed something curious. The attic turned at the far corner, leaving a small space that was easily missed. The space would be right about where her bedroom was, maybe even right over her bed. Frowning, Mary clutched her flashlight a little tighter and forged ahead.

As soon as she turned the corner, she yelped in surprise. Her flashlight fell upon a human figure standing dead center in the beam. The figure froze, like it was expecting her to attack. Mary realized that she wasn't looking at a person at all, but an old mannequin. Whoever had propped it up here must have had a really strange sense of humor.

Mary chuckled at herself. Maybe she'd been expecting a mouse after all. She breathed a sigh of relief and turned back to the attic hatch, stumbling right into the person who'd been standing just behind her.

Mary screamed. She had just enough time to register the figure's brown skin, dark shoulder-length hair, and strong chin. They

were her own features—a distorted and nightmarishly gleeful version of her own face. Then her flashlight went dead.

In the confusion that followed, Mary felt slender fingers struggling to grasp her legs. She kicked with all her might and connected with something unpleasantly soft, like a vegetable that was going to rot. Breaking free of the grasping hands, she scrambled toward the open hatch leading back to the hallway, the light filtering up providing her only illumination. She had almost reached the edge when the ladder and trapdoor swung up on their own, slamming into the frame with a deafening boom. From the darkness behind Mary came a soft, wet chuckling sound—followed by the noise of something slowly slithering toward her.

Mary pushed against the trapdoor as hard as she could, hoping to force her way out, but it was firmly stuck in place. All the while, the horrific noises behind her drew closer. The flashlight flickered with a life of its own. Each strobe of light briefly illuminated the creature making its way toward her.

Though it had once looked just like Mary, it was clear that she'd caught its head in one of her desperate kicks. Mary's own familiar features were now dented and sagging on the creature's skull. But the monster kept laughing as it approached, and it moved with a terrifying slowness.

Finally, in a last desperate effort, Mary stood right on the trapdoor—and jumped as hard as she could. Before she knew it, she was tumbling into the light of the upstairs hallway and landing hard on her back.

She lay there, stunned, as a long, strange arm reached out from the void above and slowly pulled the trapdoor shut. It made a soft click as it slid seamlessly back into the ceiling. Mary could still hear the sounds of muffled laughter from within. *There is no denying it now,* she thought. *Beacon Point has monsters.*

CHAPTER TWELVE
BABYSITTERS CLUB

"There's an animal in our yard," said Kyle Roth.

He'd been gazing out the front window, bored nearly out of his mind, when his eye had caught something moving fast around the side of the house.

"What do you mean, an animal?" his sitter Jennifer asked. "Like a dog?"

"Just, like, an animal. I didn't see it for long enough. But why can't you believe me when I say something? You don't have to assume I'm lying."

Jennifer sighed. But honestly, what else was new? She always seemed annoyed by Kyle these days, no matter what he did.

Jennifer had been babysitting him on and off for the last couple of years now. While he used to love playing games and watching movies with her, recently he'd felt irritated by her presence. She

was less fun and more preoccupied with boring stuff like safety. And she seemed more interested in her own teenage world than she was in Kyle. Well, if she didn't want to be here, why should he want her to be here, either?

The evening had actually started off okay, too. Jennifer had arrived and exchanged pleasantries with Mom and Dad at the door. But once they left, the mood had quickly soured.

He was so bored, he'd been forced to give her a hard time on purpose. It was all he could do to get some excitement!

While Jennifer had been paying the pizza guy, Kyle broke a couple of plates setting up for dinner. And right off the bat, she'd assumed he'd done it on purpose! The fact that he *had* was completely beside the point. Where was the benefit of the doubt? Ever since then, Jennifer had been watching him like a hawk, making sure he did his homework instead of playing games on his phone. The boredom had returned with reinforcements.

Perhaps it made sense that she'd be suspicious. Making up some animal outside just to keep things interesting was certainly something he'd do—but this time, it was the truth! Whatever it was had been quick, but Kyle definitely saw the blur of motion as something ran past the house on all fours. It was too fast to make out any details, though, aside from a general shape and the direction it had been headed.

"Let me see." Jennifer crouched next to Kyle on the couch to look out the living room window. "Where is it now?"

The suburban landscape laid out before them was scenic. Past the Roths' lush green lawn, the street was empty, lit by little islands of light from each streetlamp. Kyle's family lived in a nicer part of Beacon Point, all trimmed lawns and gated fences. The houses across from them were mostly dark, with the occasional flickering blue light from a TV illuminating a living room window. Kyle observed the branches of the old oak next to the driveway sway in the cool night wind. When he turned with excitement to see what Jennifer thought about the possibility of a wild animal nearby, he found she was about to turn away.

She didn't believe him at all. In fact, she looked ready to banish him to his room for the rest of the night.

"Listen, I know it's fun to make up stories, but I think it's time to head to bed before your parents—"

"There! Look!"

Before she could finish, Kyle saw another flash of movement from whatever animal was lurking outside.

And by the look on Jennifer's face, he could tell she'd seen it, too. Something *was* out there moving, sliding behind the oak tree in the yard. But before either of them could get a good look, whatever it was had shifted out of sight again.

"That was . . . probably just the wind blowing some trash around," Jennifer said. "Let's just take it easy, okay?"

He scoffed. "You don't expect me to believe that, do you? It's probably a deer from the woods! I wanna go outside and see!"

As he headed for the front door, Jennifer moved to stop him.

"Kyle, please, come on. You gotta go to bed."

Kyle crossed his arms and leaned against the kitchen wall. Let her think she'd won, and it'd be much easier to sneak outside on his own.

"What'll you give me if I do?"

Jennifer sighed and rubbed her eyes. "Fine, you little gremlin. What do you want?"

"Ice cream bar. The good ones Dad keeps at the back of the freezer."

"No way, man. The last thing you need is more sugar."

"Dr Pepper, then."

"Again, not happening. I'm trying to get you to go to sleep, not so hyper you stay up until dawn."

"I'll drink a diet one."

Jennifer smirked. "Only if it's not caffeinated."

"Fine, fine."

"Sold, then. I'll bring it to you upstairs. You can chug the thing. Then make sure you brush your teeth, okay?"

Kyle marched triumphantly upstairs. But just because he said he was going to go to bed, that didn't mean he'd stay there, not just yet. He had to get a look at the animal in the yard before it left!

After his victory soda and perfunctory toothbrushing, Kyle waited until he was sure that Jennifer was downstairs again. Then he shoved a sweater in his school backpack and slowly opened the bedroom door. He crept past the bathroom and into his parents' bedroom, careful to avoid all the soft spots in the carpet where the floorboards creaked. Once there, he grabbed the little windup safety flashlight his parents kept on hand. This past summer, blackouts had been increasingly frequent, so most families had a flashlight or two close by.

Kyle watched from the top of the stairs as Jennifer puttered in the kitchen. She was getting something from the fridge—the spill of cold light highlighted her red hair and hoodie. He took a breath, held it, and then started to move. He crept across the landing and downstairs, then made his way toward the back door. Kyle opened it just enough to slip through and quietly let it fall back into place.

He figured he only had a little bit of time before Jennifer caught on that he was no longer in his room, and he intended to make the most of it. Kyle trudged a short way away from the back door, toward the small tangle of dark woods bordering their property, before deciding it was safe to switch on his flashlight. Even still, he covered the end with his palm and kept it pointed toward his chest—ready in case he needed it. He walked a bit farther out and quietly hopped the small fence that separated his backyard from the shadowy trees. Safely obscured, Kyle briefly uncovered his flashlight and shone it around. Caught in the beam of light, the branches in the trees moved like waving arms, sending a spattering of leaves down to crunch under his feet.

Slowly moving the light back and forth, he suddenly caught a patch of reddish-brown fur between two trees. It disappeared before he could even react, however, moving deeper into the forest. Then Kyle heard shouting from behind him.

"Kyle! Kyle, come back right now!" Jennifer yelled. This was followed by the sounds of her footsteps in the leaves as she broke into a run.

It wasn't fair! Just as he was about to see what he *knew* was a deer, Jennifer would haul him back home and make him stay cooped up in his room for the rest of the night. He couldn't let it happen.

Kyle took off running in the direction the deer had gone, moving quickly to stay ahead of Jennifer. He ducked under a low branch, wincing as it snagged some of his shaggy brown hair, and did his best to avoid the tough roots jutting up from the under-brush. They seemed to grab at his feet, hoping to trip him up and break an ankle.

"Kyle! Please!" Jennifer shouted in the near distance. "Wait a minute!"

Suddenly, he had an idea. He turned off his flashlight and ducked into a stand of wild shrubbery. He made sure he was tucked as far out of sight as possible, pulling some dead branches in after him. Then he waited.

A moment later Jennifer came bounding by, her worn sneakers visible for only a second as she moved farther up the path. Just because she was older than him, Jennifer thought she knew better, but not this time.

Kyle stayed where he was. He closed his eyes for a moment, just listening to the wind blowing through the branches. Quietly, he started counting, hoping that Jennifer was still moving up the path and away from his hiding spot.

"One. Two. Three. Four. Fi—"

A branch snapped from very close nearby.

Kyle opened his eyes. Just a couple of yards in front of him stood the tall and graceful form of an adult deer, cast in silhouette by the moonlight shining down onto the rough forest path behind it. It hadn't seemed to notice him in his hiding spot yet! This was the perfect opportunity. Moving slowly, so as not to scare it off before the time was right, Kyle turned on his flashlight. He scanned up the thin, branch-like limbs to the delicately furred torso, a vibrant red-brown, before settling the beam onto the deer's face.

Kyle screamed. The face now turning curiously in his direction was horrifically wrong. It was the pale and waxy face of a human corpse, warped almost beyond recognition. As it took its first step in his direction, its mouth dropped open and the deer let out a low, rumbling moan. Kyle felt it as if it were a physical force pulling at his chest.

Stumbling to his feet, Kyle took off like a shot. The path seemed to stretch away from him as he ran, becoming strange and hostile. Branches slapped at his face and exposed hands, drawing thin trails of blood, and thorns tore at his clothes. He ran for what felt like hours but was probably only moments before he was forced to stop and catch his breath.

He wondered where Jennifer was. Had she encountered that horrible monster, too? He wiped a sheen of sweat from his forehead and bent over his knees. He'd somehow ended up in a small clearing, bordered on all sides by trees. Despite being so close to his house, this area was completely unfamiliar. How had the clearing been here the whole time, and Kyle had never stumbled upon it?

Then—a rustling from the tree line. Kyle watched as the brush parted and another of those awful things stepped gingerly toward him. This one had long patchy hair that fell over its eyes and a single twisted antler that corkscrewed out of its skull. He backed away in a panic. All around him, he heard the moans of more of those monsters approaching.

Emerging from the trees, the deer that weren't deer surrounded him in a wide circle. Kyle nearly tripped over a root before catching his balance. He turned toward the direction he thought led toward home. Three of the creatures stood in his path, their gruesome silhouettes stark in the moonlight. Kyle braced himself; he was going to have to get around them one way or another.

He took a deep breath—then burst headlong at the closest creature in his path. At the last second before impact, Kyle swerved left, narrowly avoiding a descending hoof. For once, his small size was paying off!

Seeing an opening, he moved past the other two and broke into a full sprint. If he could make it back to the house, he'd have the relative safety of a closed door between him and those . . . things. Most importantly, he could call for help! Jennifer was still out here in the woods somewhere! He had to call someone. He could—

But the thought was broken off as his feet tangled beneath him. Before he knew it, Kyle was sliding to a stop as a dusty heap on the trail, with the sounds of approaching monsters close behind.

CHAPTER THIRTEEN
THROUGH THE WOODS

Jennifer was lost. She'd followed Kyle into the woods in another attempt to keep him from getting into trouble, but the trees all looked the same under the cover of darkness. It wasn't long before she'd gotten turned around.

"Kyle! Kyle, answer me, okay?" Jennifer shouted at the crowd of trees. "This isn't funny anymore."

Her only answer was a gust of wind that rattled the branches above, setting a few leaves spiraling to the ground.

This was bad. If she didn't find Kyle soon, what would she say to his parents?

Oh, he ran out into the scary woods at night and disappeared forever! Sorry about that!

Jennifer balled her fists in frustration. Once again, she told herself that this was the last babysitting job she'd ever take. The pitifully small amount of money she earned for each night of concentrated chaos was no longer worth it, if it had ever been.

She sucked in breath to call for Kyle again but stopped when she heard someone crying out nearby. The shout was weakened by distance, but it was unmistakably that of a little boy. Jennifer recognized real fear in that cry.

"Kyle!" she shouted. Pausing only to pick up an old branch at her feet, she turned in the direction of the cry and took off like a bolt. Jennifer tried to keep her shoulders squared and her head tucked down to avoid the worst of the branches, but quite a few slapped at her as she ran. She didn't notice the thick, low-hanging branch until it was too late.

It whipped her across the forehead like a plank. Jennifer stumbled back, raising a hand to her forehead, and felt a small trickle of blood. Then she heard the cry again. It was definitely Kyle, and he was much closer now.

As Jennifer pushed on, she realized that none of this felt right. She'd been in the woods behind Kyle's house before, when the two of them would hunt for birds or bugs. The trees had never been this close together. It felt like the branches were *trying* to hinder her progress, as if the entire forest was out to get her. Jennifer pushed through the last of the bushes. Suddenly, an open field stretched before her. She'd found some kind of circular clearing.

In the middle of this space was a small, prone figure in jeans and a T-shirt. Kyle! But he wasn't alone.

The boy was surrounded on all sides by deer, their slim brown bodies pushing toward him as he crawled backward in terror. What was going on here? Glancing at the nearest animal, Jennifer had to stop herself from screaming as she saw the head that topped the delicate deer body. The patchy red-brown fur on the deer's neck gave way to sagging, pale skin, terminating in an oblong head that looked utterly wrong and unnatural. With a shock, Jennifer realized that *all* the animals wore the ghastly faces of human corpses, their jaws slack and their eyes dull and whited over.

But she only had seconds before one of the creatures was right on top of Kyle. She needed to act fast. Tightening her hold on the branch, Jennifer moved in behind the nearest monster. They were so focused on Kyle that they hadn't noticed her yet.

"Hey, uglies!" Jennifer yelled. "Leave him alone!"

Raising the thick branch in both hands like a club, Jennifer took a giant swing at the closest monster. Its nightmarish head buckled, sending the deer spilling to the side with a horrific crunch. The rest of the creatures paused, their attention now fully on her.

Jennifer made her way slowly to Kyle in the center of the clearing, brandishing her weapon for all to see. Kyle was just standing as she arrived.

"I'm so sorry I snuck out!" he said. "I had no idea—"

"Save it, okay?" Jennifer whispered, cutting him off. "When I say run, you run for the house as fast as you can. Once we're inside, we'll lock the door and call for help."

As Jennifer spoke, the nearest deer looked on and a wretched smile spread across its drooping face. It stepped forward and was just stretching its neck out to bite onto Kyle's coat when Jennifer spun and bashed the creature in the forehead as hard as she could. The white flesh of the creature's head seemed to mold inward under the weight of the branch. It made a strange bleating sound in response, but already seemed to be recovering.

"Run!" she shouted at the top of her lungs. Jennifer pushed past the dazed creature with Kyle in tow. The two sprinted toward the house, the moans of the creatures echoing behind them. By the thuds of their hooves in the earth, it sounded like the full herd was chasing them now, ripping through the underbrush and snapping branches under their powerful limbs.

But it wasn't long before Jennifer and Kyle reached the fence that separated the Roth residence from the surrounding forest. Jennifer wasted no time. She picked Kyle up and all but tossed him over the fence, before jumping for a handhold herself. Then she quickly pulled her scrambling legs over the divider. In another heartbeat they were both inside and Jennifer was dead-bolting the door.

She ran to the kitchen phone and was already dialing 911 before she realized that she wasn't getting a dial tone. Instead, the receiver pressed to her ear was emitting a garbled stream of noise that resembled radio static. Jennifer listened closely, fascinated by the odd tones. She thought she could hear a voice in the static, a few desperate words hidden under the distortion.

"Please . . . radio . . . turn . . . it off . . . I'm so sorry . . ." the voice said, almost too weak to hear.

"Is something wrong with the phone?" Kyle asked in a near panic. "Jennifer?"

Jennifer listened with an eerie focus. As she did, Kyle turned back to the window that faced the backyard and gasped. Jennifer snapped out of her daze and dropped the phone, leaving it to dangle on its wire. All the deer were outside, an entire herd. They stood in a loose line at the back fence, facing the house. It was hard to hear from behind the glass, but their faces seemed to be contorted in wild laughter.

As they watched, the animal things moved leisurely closer, taking their time. And even more of the creatures were emerging from behind the dense cover of the forest. Lit by the pale light of the moon, their nightmarish faces were on stark display. All wore the distorted faces of human beings, some men and some women. A few were even children, their small human heads balanced on the

long and graceful necks of fawns. Some had antlers, though horrifically malformed. They grew oddly from the fronts or backs of the deer's heads.

"Wh-what are we going to do, Jennifer?" Kyle stammered. "Can they get in?"

Jennifer turned, searching for another exit. If the deer surrounded the house, they'd be trapped here without any way of calling for help. She was about to suggest they escape out the front door while the monsters were busy at the back when the TV clicked on, seemingly on its own.

The empty living room was suddenly awash in the bright glow of static as the air was filled with a strange noise—the same sound Jennifer had heard coming from the phone only moments before. It reminded her of the static you would find between stations on a radio. The noise grew in volume and intensity, until both Jennifer and Kyle had to cover their ears. Just as it was becoming too much to bear, the TV switched off again, and the house was blanketed in quiet.

In the distance, a dog barked. A lone car alarm rang out into the night, and then was silent. The night was strangely still.

"Kyle, look . . ." Jennifer said, pointing to the window.

The backyard was empty. The animals were gone, as if they'd never been there in the first place. Beyond the fence, the forest loomed. To Jennifer, it looked like it was inviting them to leave the safety of their house and venture down its winding paths once again.

Ep. 34
"Weird Deer, Pt. 1"
Partial transcript of the
BCON RADIO MYSTERY SHOW,
hosted by Alan Graves

Broadcast on March 10, 1994

[Atmospheric eerie music plays]

Alan Graves: Longtime listeners will
remember our ongoing series of reports
on the strange animals often seen in
the nearby woods, the elusive not-deer,
as they've come to be known among an
especially devoted section of our fans!
These odd creatures have been sighted on
multiple occasions throughout the history
of our fair town. In one of our previous
episodes, we mentioned that in 1904, a
group of hunters led by one Nathaniel
Raymere came upon some trouble while

pursuing a herd of deer that called the area home. Nathaniel was something of an outcast in the then-small village, living away from town and generally being known as an eccentric. He claimed to receive supernatural visions that showed him the past, and sometimes even the future, of Beacon Point. Though these supposed visions were never clear enough to help change his luck—poor Nathaniel! Instead, he alleged that he received strange images and phrases, and shared just enough for most folks to think him a weirdo. Adding to his troubles, Nathaniel was quite poor. He often relied on the kindness of the other villagers to keep a full belly.

But one winter, the village was hit hard. Harvests had been lean, and the woods seemed empty of wild game. All the finest hunters in the village went out, but aside from the rare rabbit, every single one came back empty-handed. In addition to that horrible luck, all the food that had been prepared to survive the coming cold months was found to have mysteriously gone bad.

And as the story goes, the night they
discovered the food had gone foul,
Nathaniel was gifted with the clearest
vision he'd ever seen.

He saw an area of the forest that none
ever hunted overflowing with deer. It was
just waiting for him to come along and
snare enough food to save his village.
No longer would he be an outcast among
his own people; Nathaniel would become
the celebrated hero who had delivered his
neighbors from the clutches of starvation.

The next day, Nathaniel was in the town
square bright and early, calling for the
finest hunters to gather and hear what he
had to say. Nathaniel told them that he had
received a message from God that would
surely save them all, about an area of land
where the hunting was bountiful. There was
enough food to survive until the spring, if
only they would go out and take it.

And while many were skeptical of
Nathaniel's claims, it wasn't long before
four of the hunters agreed to join his
venture. As with many in the village, there

were folk who had previously hunted the woods and come back empty-handed.

Nathaniel assured them that, according to his vision, there was no way they could go wrong. But they had to hurry. It wouldn't be long before the season's snowfall started and they'd be up to their ears in it.

So the hunting party decided to head out the very next day. They raided their meager storehouse for a week's provisions, though they didn't expect to be out that long.

Little did those five men know as they disappeared into the darkness of the trees that almost none of them would ever see their homes again.

[End of broadcast]

CHAPTER FOURTEEN
THE BASEMENT

Rebecca sat in the dark basement, working at the pang of anxiety now knotted inside her. She'd spent her lunch hour in a very public argument with her friend Amber. The whole thing had put her in such a bad mood that she had no choice but to skip the rest of her classes for the day.

Their friend Jeremy was missing, and as she was the last one to see him, Amber had blamed *her* for his disappearance. As if Rebecca had kidnapped him or something!

Jeremy had disappeared on his way home, after rushing out of Rebecca's living room in a hurried goodbye. The whole thing was horrible. Rebecca felt so overwhelmed—escaping to her basement hideout seemed like the best way to clear her head.

In the south side of town, not far from her school, there was an old factory that had been condemned for as long as she could remember. Last year during her summer break, Rebecca had been biking around town with nothing to do and decided to explore the area. It was here that she'd found the hideout. At the back of the main factory, right against the tree line, was a small, separate building little bigger than a garage. Most of the windows were boarded up, but Rebecca had found an unblocked one at ground level toward the back that led into an underground space. After pressing her way through the vegetation and trees that crowded the area, she'd bashed it open with a few well-aimed kicks. Checking to make sure no one had heard the commotion, she then crouched down and slipped her legs through.

Inside, it was another world. Despite its many years of neglect, the space was clean and cool, with a concrete floor. It didn't look like a factory at all. Perhaps it had been a storage space?

Well, whoever had been the owner at one time, it was clear that it was all hers now. The window was the only way in or out, as someone had barricaded what she presumed was the corridor to the upper floor. The summer heat couldn't reach her here, and she felt strangely protected by the room's inky shadows. It was peaceful and private—a privacy that Rebecca wasn't used to. She'd ended up visiting many times. Eventually, she started bringing in modest pieces of furniture like the small mattress her neighbors were giving away, along with a flashlight and lots of reading material. It was nice.

Perhaps *hideout* wasn't the most appropriate name for the room, but it was the first thing that had popped into Rebecca's head when she saw it, and so it had stuck.

Whenever things got to her, she could come here to be alone, to let the stress fade a little. School was hard at the best of times;

Rebecca often found herself in fights. It was never anything that she pursued. The older kids just seemed to focus their wrath on her, and she had no choice but to defend herself. They loved to tease her about how tall she was, or her thick black hair and the spattering of freckles spread across her face. Things had only gotten worse when she started getting pimples.

The adults were no use. Rebecca inevitably got in trouble when she defended herself. It was nice to have a place to just . . . disappear for a while.

As the weather changed and the warmth of summer slowly gave way to the chill of autumn, Rebecca had meant to stop going to the hideout, at least until next spring.

But the fight with Amber had been a special kind of betrayal. Rebecca was so worried for Jeremy. He was one of the few kids who treated her kindly! That her friend would throw his disappearance in her face like that . . . She just had to escape.

Today, however, she was quickly finding the hideout wasn't quite the escape she'd hoped for. Previously, solitude had been one of the qualities she loved best about it. Now it gave her the creeps. The shadows had a quality that they'd never had before, pools of black that were broken by the thin shaft of light angling in through the window.

Rebecca had only been here for a half hour or so, but she was already debating whether to head home in time for dinner. Eventually, her parents would stop believing her excuse about staying out too late with friends. Like every parent in Beacon Point, they had a real hang-up about kids staying out after the sun went down. Especially after Jeremy . . .

"Definitely time to go, I think!" she exclaimed to no one, but the sound of her voice broke the gathered silence and made her feel a little better.

Rebecca collected books and magazines, along with the chip bags and soda cans she had emptied while there. Then she walked toward the little window that served as entrance and exit, and pushed it with all her weight.

Nothing. The window, which had never given her any trouble in the past, was solidly stuck in place.

Rebecca pushed again, then once more, but still nothing. Rebecca had broken the lock when she first found her way in here, yet the panel stayed firmly shut. Just past the smudged glass, she could see the front wheel and handlebar of her bike. It was so close to her, but completely beyond her reach. She took a step back, making a low, frustrated noise.

Thump.

Upstairs a heavy footstep reverberated. Then a second.

"Hello?" Rebecca yelled to whoever was there. "Hello! Can you help? I think I'm stuck down here!"

The footsteps slowly made their way across the wooden floor, coming to rest directly above her. Whoever was up there must have heard her. But why didn't they respond?

Suddenly, Rebecca was having second thoughts about making herself known to the stranger. She backed into the nearest corner, away from where the footsteps had stopped, and stayed quiet. Rebecca swore to herself that when she eventually got out of here, she was never coming back. The hideout had forever lost its appeal.

Something caught her eye, the fading light glinting off an

object protruding from the ceiling. Removing her flashlight from her pack, Rebecca aimed it upward. Whatever it was, it was small. She thought absurdly of some strange glittering insect.

But as the beam of light landed, Rebecca screamed.

Growing right from the concrete ceiling were five long, withered fingers. The index finger wore a plain silver ring that had caught the rays of the setting sun. Even as Rebecca watched, the fingers dug themselves from the concrete as if by magic, revealing a pale, rotten-looking hand and then an arm. Next to it, five more fingers pushed through the solid surface.

Rebecca watched, transfixed, as a long, curved form began to emerge from the ceiling. Though its arms appeared human, as its head materialized, Rebecca was shocked to recognize the oversized

head of a crow. Its curved beak glinted in the half-light of the basement.

It was only when the creature's bone-white eyes rolled in her direction that the spell was broken. Rebecca burst toward the window, screaming and striking at the glass with the base of her flashlight, over and over.

Behind her, something soft and rotten dropped in a fetid bundle to the basement floor—a mass of black mold and decayed cloth.

But Rebecca kept up her barrage on the glass, and soon cracks began to appear, stretching from the point where she struck with her flashlight. Tears streaming down her face, she heard fabric shifting behind her as the bird thing stood to its full height.

She refused to turn around, just swung the flashlight again and again until, finally, the glass exploded outward.

Rebecca knocked a few errant shards away with her coat, then dove headfirst through the little window, her legs still hanging in the basement. She felt the brush of cold air on her ankles as something tried to grab her feet, but yanked herself through the window with a scream. Rebecca grabbed up her bike and pushed it through the brush, branches smacking her face and swiping at her hands.

Soon she was on it, pedaling for the road as fast as she could, still refusing to look back.

If she had, she'd have seen eyes like white marbles reflecting the last light of dusk, and a beak as sharp as a sickle.

CHAPTER FIFTEEN
NO SUCH THING

Mary was barely keeping it together after her encounter in the attic.

She'd told her parents about an intruder—had even gotten them to call the police—but that had led nowhere. A couple of bored-looking police officers came to their door and took down their information, but Mary could sense they didn't believe a word she said.

Mary had claimed it was a burglar. She knew that if she said a monster had attacked her, they would have dismissed her outright. Still, after scouring every inch of the musty old attic, her dad said that if someone had been up here, they were long gone now. The dust was undisturbed and the furniture looked like it hadn't been moved in years.

The more likely scenario, her dad said, was that she'd gone

up there by herself and gotten spooked. While investigating, he'd called her over to the hidden far corner.

"What is it?" Mary said. "Did you find the burglar?"

"I might have. Come take a look."

Mary slowly walked over to where her dad was pointing his flashlight and gasped as it landed on the eerie mannequin. Then she bristled at the implication.

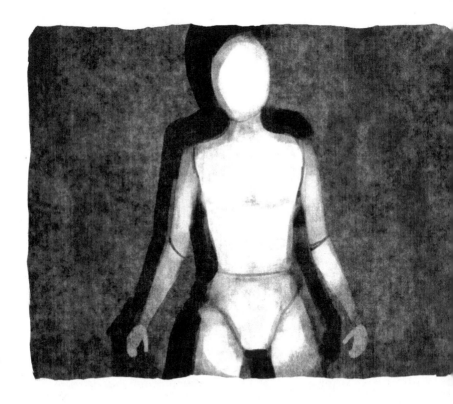

"Dad, I know what a mannequin is. This wasn't the . . . person who attacked me. I barely escaped!"

"I know, I know. You were up here, in the dark, all by yourself!

Anybody would have been scared! But there's nothing here now, right? Can we agree on that?" He swept the flashlight across the barren space.

"Yeah," Mary conceded in a small voice. "Let's just . . . Let's get out of here before all this dust gets to me."

Her dad meant well, but it was going to be tough to convince him that she'd seen anyone upstairs, much less a monster wearing her face.

She thought again of the odd boy at school, Byron. He'd said that Beacon Point was some kind of monster hot spot. Maybe he knew more about the creature she had seen. She had to find him again. If she and her family were in danger, then she needed to know everything he did.

So the next day at school, Mary spent every moment outside class looking for that familiar oversized coat and those giant glasses. It was impossible to focus on her classwork, anyway. She'd stayed up all night, afraid the monster would reappear. Thankfully, the scratching sound never returned. It might be gone for now, whatever it was, but Mary felt sure it would be back. And if it could leave the attic, what was to stop it from crawling into her bedroom while she slept? Or her parents' room?

Finally tuning in to the English lesson unfolding in front of her—the whiteboard was half covered in grammar instructions—Mary raised her hand and asked Ms. Simmons if she could use the bathroom.

"Of course, Mary," Ms. Simmons said, already turning back to the board. "Just hurry back, all right?"

Outside, it was exceedingly quiet. Mary made her way down to the bottom floor, where the closest public restrooms were located. She was about to push her way into the girls' room when she heard hushed voices whispering from the boys' next door.

Slowly, so as not to disturb whoever was talking, she eased the door open and looked in. Inside, several different students were draped over the bathroom counter and leaning against stall doors. They seemed to be in the middle of an intense conversation—but were trying to keep their voices down.

"It's just like that radio show," said a reedy voice that she immediately recognized as Byron's. "Everything you guys have talked about, Alan Graves has covered on his show. I think he's trying to warn us. Monsters are attacking people—attacking kids—all across town, and he's the only adult who believes in them."

"Well, *I* believe," said another voice. "After what I saw."

Leaning in, Mary was surprised to see that the second voice belonged to Lucas, the other boy who'd sat with her at lunch. He'd seemed so skeptical the other day, but now his face was dead serious. He ran his fingers through his blond mullet and looked lost in thought.

"It was in the field outside my house. The scarecrow, my family's scarecrow . . . was moving. Alive. Then it attacked me. When I ran from it, it fell apart into a mass of bugs." Lucas leaned against the back wall, his arms crossed over his lanky frame.

Along with the two boys, there was a slightly older girl with shoulder-length red hair, and a girl around Mary's age with thick black hair and a face covered in freckles.

"Look," said Byron as he jumped up to sit on the bathroom sink behind him. "Over the last week or so, we've all had an encounter with the supernatural in this town. I saw the man in the long coat. Rebecca encountered that bird thing near that factory on the south side of town."

The girl with thick black hair shuddered. "I know how it sounds, but it came out of the ceiling," she insisted.

"I believe you," Byron said. "Whatever it was, it wasn't normal. And we've all seen something like it."

Mary stepped fully into the room and cleared her throat.

"I've seen something, too," she said. She watched as all the kids' heads turned in her direction at once. "Mary!" Byron exclaimed, hopping to his feet. "Nice to see you again. I was going to find you at lunch and ask if you'd encountered anything paranormal. You have, then?"

"In my attic," Mary said, nodding. "Something that can look like me. I don't care what it is. What I want to know is, what are we going to do about it? My parents don't believe me. The cops don't believe me, either. But it could come back at any time."

"We're not just talking about one or two monsters," said the redheaded girl. "There's a whole army of them lurking in the woods! Kyle—the kid I babysit—he and I both saw them. They almost got us. We went to the police and they basically laughed us out of the room."

"What we need is proof," Byron said. "If we can get that, then we can convince the adults in this town that what's happening is real."

"There's one other thing," said Jennifer slowly. "The other night, when we were cornered by those monsters at Kyle's house, we tried to call for help. But the phone was full of static. There was a voice asking for help. It mentioned something about a radio."

"There's a radio station on the far side of town, right?" Mary asked. "Up on that peak. I saw it as we drove in."

"Yeah, that's the only local station I've ever heard of," said Lucas. He turned to Byron. "I know Alan Graves is like your buddy, but is there any chance he's *involved* in this?"

"He's not my buddy," Byron said defensively. "I just like his program, okay? It's interesting!"

"Well, it's something to keep in mind," Rebecca said. "Maybe we should go snoop around up there, see what's up?"

By the excited gleam in Rebecca's eye, Mary could tell that sneaking around old buildings was something that appealed to the girl.

Lucas spoke up again. "Tomorrow night, my dad's going out of town for a couple days. I'll be on my own. Why don't we gather everything we need, tell our parents it's a sleepover, and we can do a monster stakeout together. Most of these things have been sighted from the woods, which are pretty close to me. Maybe, if we look as a group, we'll catch something and get some photos . . . And there's safety in numbers, right?"

"Wait, you want US to find THEM?" Jennifer said. "Are you serious?" She looked at Lucas like he'd just suggested they all jump off a cliff.

"Hey, I'm just exploring our options here!" Lucas said, his face flushing. "We get a snapshot of one of these things, someone will help us."

The room was silent for a moment before Byron spoke up.

"I think that's a great idea," he said. "A reconnaissance

operation! We know we need proof, and this is better than being picked off separately."

One by one, the other kids agreed to gather supplies, tell their parents they were staying with a friend (not exactly a lie), and then make their way to Lucas's farm after school the next day.

"If it keeps me and my parents safe, I'm all for it," Mary said.

Now all that was left was to prepare.

Ep. 35
"Weird Deer, Pt. 2"
Partial transcript of the
BCON RADIO MYSTERY SHOW,
hosted by Alan Graves

Broadcast on March 17, 1994

Alan Graves: It was only two days after Nathaniel Raymere led his hunting party into the forest that he was seen reemerging from the woods. Witnesses described him stumbling into town around twilight, all but delirious. Much of his clothing now hung in rags, his thin arms and face bloodied. Once they had brought him in from the cold and fed him a meager bowl of broth, the dazed look started to fade from his eyes and he recounted the tale of what had happened to his doomed party.

According to Nathaniel, the group had started out in great spirits, convinced of his vision of the bounty awaiting them. The

men had brought a couple of immense sleds
that they dragged behind them, to help
transport the meat back to the village.

The journey out to that unexplored patch
of woods was long, but the group traded
stories and sang songs to pass the time.
Before long, it was time to make camp
for the night.

They assembled a roaring fire, cooked a
meager dinner. Nathaniel sat away from the
rest of the men, his long hair hanging
in his face, content to listen to the
experienced hunters tell their tall tales.

That night, Nathaniel claimed he was
woken from a fitful sleep by the sound
of a branch snapping. Rising, he saw
the silhouette of a massive figure at the
edge of their camp. Immense antlers
were outlined against a darker field of
black. Before he could alert the other
men, however, the stag turned and darted
silently into the deeper brush.

But Nathaniel took this as a sign of good
fortune. They were on the right path. It

wouldn't be long before they had enough food to feed their village.

However, the next morning the group woke up to a forest that felt . . . different. More ominous than the woods they'd gone to sleep in. The trees had lost all their leaves seemingly overnight, and the bright sky of the day before was now gray and churning. Pale, thick vines now grew around many of the tree trunks, as if trying to strangle them.

Nathaniel told the hunters of the massive elk. But where he had seen the animal as a good omen, the others felt it was a bad sign. Some were furious with Nathaniel for not waking them to hunt the creature down. Gone were the high spirits and tall tales. Now the hunters marched in silence, dragging their sleds behind them.

And as they finally reached the area of the forest Nathaniel claimed to have seen in his vision, the men started to hear things. Odd noises drifted from far back among the trees. One hunter even swore he heard a child, though there couldn't possibly be anyone out there.

Worse yet, they didn't see any signs of wildlife, despite being careful to make as little noise as possible. The mood quickly turned frustrated. Many of the men blamed Nathaniel for dragging them into the woods and wasting precious supplies on a foolhardy hunt. But it wasn't until they all made camp again that evening that the strange atmosphere of dread exploded into violence.

Nathaniel was awoken yet again by the screams of one of the hunters, a man named Jacob. He lit a lantern just in time to see the man being dragged off into the trees by some kind of animal. But as he raised the light, Nathaniel was shocked to see a misshapen deer.

The creature's face was pale and twisted, completely without fur. Nathaniel claimed that the attacking animal had the grinning, horrible features of a human being. It had Jacob's ankle in its mouth and was backing away, pulling him step-by-step into the woods. As it did, it never broke eye contact with Nathaniel.

Watching in shock, Nathaniel realized that more of the strange animals were attacking, besieging the other hunters. Screams rang out in the dark as one by one, the men were dragged off to uncertain fates.

Soon, Nathaniel sat alone, surrounded by dark woods on all sides. He stayed that way all night, waiting for his own turn to be dragged screaming into the forest. But the attack never came. Eventually, the sun rose upon his empty camp.

After Nathaniel recounted his tale, the village sent other parties to try to recover the lost hunters. But none of the men were ever seen again. Nathaniel claimed to have no idea why he alone was spared out of the five who had marched into that foreboding foliage.

And what of the fate of the village, you ask? Well, within a week of the doomed expedition, suddenly the nearby woods were inexplicably full of rabbit, deer, and fox. It was a miracle. The town was saved from starvation for another season.

But every once in a while, a Beacon Point resident will claim to catch sight of not-deer while hiking in the woods. Some even say they recognize the faces of people who'd gone missing in the past.

Now, most accounts end the story there, but there are some who believe that Nathaniel wasn't the innocent survivor that he claimed. There are those who say that Nathaniel led those men to their dooms, fully knowing that the only way to spare the village from starvation was through sacrifice. Nathaniel's vision was not of a bountiful hunting ground but a forbidden—and hungry—patch of woods.

Of course, we'll never know for sure, dear listener. But it's fun to think about, right? Oh, and that dark forest where the hunters were attacked? Why, those are the North Woods of our own Beacon Point. So the next time you're thinking about

a solo nature walk, think of Nathaniel
and his not-deer, and bring a friend. Or
perhaps . . . a sacrifice?

Until next time, lovely listeners, stay
safe out there!

[Atmospheric eerie music plays]

[BG SFX: Lightning crashes, owl hoots]

[End of broadcast]

CHAPTER SIXTEEN
FRIENDS

When Mary came home that day, her parents were busy repainting the living room. Wide swaths of bright teal were slowly swallowing up the dusty eggshell walls.

Her father turned as she took off her boots. He was wearing a paint-splattered undershirt and torn jeans, paint roller in hand.

"Hey!" he said. "How was school? Care to join your parents as they tirelessly beautify your new abode?" He crossed his sweaty arms and grinned.

"I'd really love to help, Dad," Mary said, "but I honestly don't have time. I need to get ready! I'm staying over at a friend's house tomorrow evening and I want to get all my stuff packed as soon as possible."

"A friend!" Her mom perked up. "Already? Wow, you're making the best of this place in no time!" She'd obviously been a little less careful with her painting than Dad; a splotch of teal decorated her forehead above the right eyebrow.

"What, is it such a big surprise that I have friends now?" Mary asked. "I'm very likable, I'll have you know." She took in the chaos that was their living room. "Well, this looks fun and all, but I'll catch you both later. I'll be in my room. Don't bug me until dinner!"

At that, Mary cut off whatever her parents might have said to her as she bounded up the stairs to her room. She couldn't help but eye the hatch to the attic warily as she made her way down the hall. Her parents had secured the edges of the door with layers of thick duct tape, just to make her feel slightly safer. At the very least, anything escaping from that dusty alcove would have to make a ton of noise.

Once she was safely away from her parents, Mary set to work. She grabbed the big red duffel bag that had held a wide selection of her favorite books for the car ride to Beacon Point, and began piling in anything she felt might be useful for an overnight monster investigation mission. She grabbed the clunky flashlight that she'd been keeping in her nightstand, a change of clothes that included a thick hoodie from her previous school, and the Swiss Army knife.

That knife had started a huge argument between her parents when she'd received it for her last birthday. Her mother had gotten it for her without telling her dad, and while Mary had thought she was ready for it, her father hadn't. There was a quiet argument behind closed doors, but in the end, Mary and her mother won out. The little candy apple–red knife was hers.

Mary also threw in a couple of bottles of water from the fridge and some snack bars for good measure, then zipped the bag up.

All across Beacon Point, she knew that Byron, Rebecca, Jennifer, and Lucas were making similar preparations. Byron was bringing a camera and his portable radio with a tape recorder in the hope that they could collect some audio or visual evidence. With that, they could convince the police, or at least their parents, that something strange was going on. Then maybe they could put an end to the kids going missing before the monsters claimed one of *them*.

Mary glanced at the ceiling over her head. If they couldn't find a way to end this, or at the very least get some help, then she suspected it was only a matter of time before the attic thing returned. And next time, Mary might not get away as easily as before.

The next day passed in a blur of classrooms, hallways, and knowing looks shared between her and the other kids. But before she knew it, Mary was being startled out of her anxious thoughts by the final school bell of the day.

In the parking lot behind the school building, Mary saw Lucas, Byron, and the others huddled in a semicircle by the bus stop. There was a new kid, too. A young boy with brown hair and wide, excited eyes.

Rebecca looked up and caught her eye, and hurriedly motioned for Mary to join them. "Mary! You made it!"

Mary nodded. "Who's this?" she said, gesturing to the boy.

"This is Kyle," sighed Jennifer. "The kid I was babysitting the night we saw the deer. His parents needed me to watch him again. The only way I could come was by promising to bring him. I'm honestly surprised they agreed. But I guess his parents know Byron's mom. When they heard he was coming, they decided it was okay, so long as *two* responsible older kids were present."

"And now you're getting paid to go on a sleepover," Kyle said. "Babysitting *rules*."

Jennifer rolled her eyes. "They're probably just relieved to be free of him for a night."

"What'd you bring?" Lucas asked Mary, gesturing to the duffel bag she'd slung over her shoulder.

"Just some odds and ends," Mary said. "I'm still not even convinced we'll find anything tonight, but it's better to be prepared." She dropped the bag to the ground at her side with a thunk.

"I brought the camera," Byron said while rooting through his own backpack. "It's got a great flash. It should work well in the dark."

"I almost got killed by that bird monster," Rebecca said, "and even *I'm* still having trouble believing this is all real. Maybe it was a hallucination or something." She stared down at her worn sneakers.

"This is real, all right," Byron said. "And tonight, we're going to prove it. Not just for us, but for all the kids who have disappeared already. Like my friend Bev."

"And Jeremy," Rebecca said, her eyes welling.

Byron nodded. "And Jeremy. And lots of other kids. Whatever took them is still out there."

As he said that, the bus pulled up beside them with a screech of brakes, startling the entire group.

"After you," said Byron, gesturing to the open door.

They all walked on and found seats. As Mary took hers and

the bus pulled away from the curb, she caught sight of a tall figure in a wide-brimmed hat at the edge of the school building, partially obscured by the foliage.

He seemed to be gazing in the direction of the bus—until it turned the corner and the figure fell out of view.

CHAPTER SEVENTEEN

SLEEPOVER

Mary, Byron, Lucas, and the rest of the group stepped out of the road as the decrepit old bus pulled away. Once deposited, they were immediately hit with a rush of foul-smelling exhaust and groaned among themselves.

The modest shops and suburban homes of Beacon Point had all been peeled away, leaving nothing but flat and barren land, surrounded by dark forest. A long, winding driveway led into the distance, where they could see a crooked two-story structure that could only be the Weaver farmhouse. Perched beside it was a beat-up old car.

Far behind the house waited the dusty field of harvested cornstalks, and beyond that, as if barely being held back, the woods started in full force. They spread across the horizon as far as anyone could see.

"C'mon, guys," Lucas said over his shoulder, already taking the lead. "My dad will be gone by now. We have the full run of the place." He started down the gravel drive, not even looking behind him.

"Fantastic," muttered Mary. "As if it wasn't spooky enough living in a haunted house, now it's time for a bonus haunted farm."

As they passed the closest field, Mary took note of the ominous figure hanging on its pole.

"That must be the scarecrow you were telling us about?" she said warily. "Mr. Sackhead? I thought it was destroyed."

Lucas paused to regard it with a look of real hatred. "It came back this morning. Dad was pleased, so I didn't push it. It seems like a regular old scarecrow again, but I'm not going anywhere near that thing. Regular scarecrows don't come back on their own."

With that said, he hurried on toward the house.

Byron watched the scarecrow with studious eyes before pulling a book from his bag and balancing it on his knee. He hastily scribbled some frantic notes, wobbling on one leg to keep his balance.

Rebecca pulled her coat a little tighter and shivered, remembering her encounter in the hideout. She prayed that staying overnight with this group was the right move. Already she was having doubts. One personal monster was bad enough. Looking up, she realized that she'd dropped behind the rest of the group, and ran to catch up. They stuck close together in a tight clump and tried their best to ignore the figure in the field until they were safely inside.

The group decided to make the living room their base of

operations, and it wasn't long before they'd each claimed a corner. Byron stretched out a camouflage-patterned sleeping bag on the floor, while Lucas took his dad's tired-looking old armchair, the one covered in little holes that stuffing was beginning to peek through.

"Well, uh, welcome to my house?" he said, his anxiety clear.

"Thanks for having us," Mary said quickly. Back home, she'd known plenty of families where money was tight. Lucas had been the first kid to introduce himself at school. He was a good person. "I wish it was under better circumstances. Mostly circumstances that don't involve evil monsters and whatnot."

Byron barked out a single note of laughter. "Can't be avoided, I guess. I hope this whole sleepover thing isn't fruitless." He had his monster manual out again and was already flipping to a new page.

"Yeah, and maybe we'll all get eaten!" Kyle said. "Have you thought of that? Each of us was attacked by different creatures, right? What if each one is hunting a particular kid, and this sleepover is like one big feast for them?"

The boy was lying on the couch with his arms crossed, a bored look on his face. Jennifer sat beside him. At that comment, she elbowed him in the side and whispered, "C'mon. You're just trying to scare everyone."

"Maybe we should be scared," Rebecca said, staring out the window at the cornfield.

The rest of the evening went smoothly, all things considered.

The atmosphere was a bit awkward, but Mary thought that was only natural. She'd barely even met most of these kids; she was still a newcomer in town.

But she found herself hoping that she could be friends with them, provided they survived the night. Leaving her old friends behind had been hard, and Mary was eager to find her footing here. That said, the only thing this group had in common so far was being attacked by monsters.

Thankfully, they had one more thing in common. Because when Lucas revealed that his dad had left money to order pizza for dinner, there was much rejoicing.

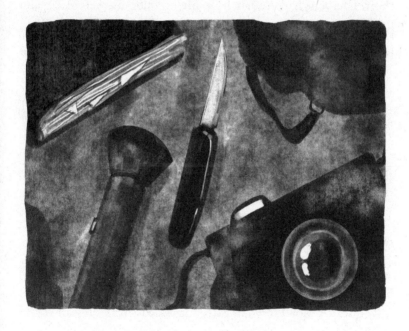

While they waited, the kids all showed off what meager supplies they'd brought for their monster-hunting expedition. Mary dumped out her duffel bag and showed off the Swiss Army knife and its modest three-inch blade. The heavy-duty flashlight she'd "borrowed" without her parents noticing might also substitute for a weapon in a pinch. It was big enough to really hurt if she, say, hit her monstrous double on the head with it.

Byron had his notebook open on the monstrous lore of Beacon Point, and he'd also brought one of the key items for the investigation—a giant, expensive-looking camera. He assured everyone again that it came equipped with a superbright flash, something that would surely come in handy once it got dark.

Aside from these things, most of the kids had come up a little short. Everyone had brought a flashlight, but none were as big and powerful as the one Mary had managed to smuggle away. Kyle had brought some trail mix from his parents' cupboard, though what that would be useful for, they weren't sure.

"I thought the deer might like it," he said, brandishing the ziplock bag full of raisins and nuts. "In case we need a distraction."

"I think those deer are only interested in eating YOU, friend," Jennifer laughed, without looking up from the magazine she was flipping through.

Suddenly, a loud buzz filled the air, causing most of the kids to jump to their feet.

Mary's heart was hammering in her chest. Had the monsters come for them already? It was barely getting dark!

Lucas settled everyone with a lopsided smile. "It's all right," he said, laughing to himself. "Even old farmhouses have doorbells. It's pizza time."

Ep. 40
"The Bird Woman of Beacon Point"
Partial Transcript of the BCON RADIO MYSTERY SHOW, hosted by Alan Graves

Broadcast on May 19, 1994

[Atmospheric eerie music plays, ravens caw, bat wing flapping SFX]

ALAN GRAVES: Hello again, dear listeners! Thank you once again for tuning in to my rancid radio show, my terror transmission. I hope that you're ready for another slice of scary small-town horror. I know I am.

Today I want to talk to you about one of the most enduringly scary entities in our town's history, the Beacon Point Bird Woman, also known as the Crow Hag, or the Crow Mother. An ancient monster that was said to haunt this land for centuries before Beacon Point was even founded. Stories abound in this neck of the woods of a creature with the enormous black-feathered head of a crow and the rotting body of a human woman, covered in moldering rags and a wretched black moss.

As the folktale goes, there was once a witch who lived in a cottage near the peak of town. And this witch's familiar, a wily old crow, discovered a method of slowly drawing power from her without her knowledge. At first it only took little bites, enough to extend its life, but then the familiar's hunger grew. Soon the crow had drained its mistress of everything she had, until it eventually killed her.

But the bird was changed. Deeply changed. Now grown to the size of a human being, it used its newfound power to live forever, preserving itself with straw and stuffing, needle and thread, and eventually learning how to replace parts of its body as they rotted. Though it had taken everything from its former mistress, now the crow took yet more, shedding its wings and talons for the witch's arms and legs.

And it still haunts the empty and abandoned places in Beacon Point to this very day, looking for new body parts to take as its own. Of course, that's just the folktale. And who'd believe such a silly old legend?

That said, there have been sightings of something like a giant bird throughout the decades, and spindly human arms reaching through windows, or even walls, to steal folks away.

One night in 1981, sixteen-year-old Ashley Baccall was babysitting in Beacon Point. No one knows exactly what happened that night, but Ashley called emergency services at 12:25 a.m. in hysterics to report that "something was reaching through the walls" and "trying to get the children."

[SFX: Woman screams, bird caws, baby crying]

By the time paramedics and police arrived, Ashley was alone, her young charges gone forever. And all she would say was that "the Crow Mother took them away."

Was there anything to her claims, or was this simply a regular old kidnapping dressed up in the ragged clothes of a spooky legend?

Over time, there have been a scant few other sightings of the Bird Woman, most famously a blurry Polaroid photo taken by one Michael Lang, a local photographer and bird-watcher.

He supposedly caught a glimpse of the monster while out one night. The photo isn't much to look at. I mean, what some would call a monstrously huge beak and grasping fingers, others might just as easily claim to be a gnarled branch and a crescent of shadow.

The jury's still out on whether Beacon Point truly is haunted by the Crow Mother, but maybe it would be best if our listeners erred on the side of caution.

Stay inside at night. Keep your lights on. And, repeat after me, avoid the woods, avoid the woods, avoid the woods! If I've ever given you dear listeners a single piece of advice to hold tightly to your heart, it would be that.

Thank you for listening once again. Tune in next time, unless the Bird Woman takes you. I'm Alan Graves, your loyal host, and I say keep digging for the truth!

[Atmospheric eerie music plays]

[BG SFX: Lightning crashes, owl hoots, bird caws]

[End of broadcast]

CHAPTER EIGHTEEN
KNOCK, KNOCK

In a moment, Lucas had the front door open and was thrusting a worn twenty-dollar bill through the crack. The startled delivery driver barely had time to grab it before the pizza had left his hands and Lucas slammed the door shut in his face.

He reentered the living room, pizza in hand, to find Byron regaling the bored-looking group with yet another local myth.

"Trust me, you guys," Byron said. "They're totally real. Giant centipedes. Living in this very area! It's more likely than you think. Tons of people around here have seen them."

Jennifer was seated to his left, just staring into the middle distance. "After what we've seen, you could tell me that Santa Claus was going door-to-door eating people alive and I'd believe you."

Lucas plopped the pizza box down on the center of the coffee table, grease already leaking through the lid, and watched as the group tore into the food. He barely got a piece for himself before all that remained was cheesy cardboard.

After they'd all digested their dinner—Kyle lying particularly still for once, in a self-induced food coma—the group settled in. Darkness had fallen in earnest by this point. The clouds effectively erased the moon from the sky, covering the farm in shadow.

"Most of the creatures strike late at night," Byron said. "So let's wait until midnight to make our sweep. Everyone can rest until then. I'll keep watch in case anything appears before then."

The rest of the group happily agreed.

He produced an oversized pair of binoculars and set them down on the windowsill in front of him, along with his monster journal and fancy camera. Rebecca sat next to Jennifer as she munched on a pizza crust and stared at the old television set propped in the corner.

"So, uh, are you doing okay?" Rebecca asked her, careful not to make eye contact.

"All things considered, pretty good! I mean, I almost got killed by some mutant deer—" Jennifer started.

"Oh, I know, right? I'm just minding my business and some weirdo with a *bird head* tries to murder me!" Rebecca exclaimed.

"—and then I'm spending my night with a bunch of kids who want to go *looking* for more trouble. I hope I don't have to fight off *too* many abominations keeping you all safe," Jennifer finished. She ran a hand through her hair, trying not to let on how worried she was.

"We may be a little younger than you, but I *know* we can take care of ourselves," Rebecca said with a smile.

"Hey, I don't doubt it!" Jennifer replied, holding up her hands as if to hold Rebecca back. "You've all survived a run-in with a monster of your own. You don't have to prove anything to me."

Satisfied by this, Rebecca turned back to the TV, though she wished she felt as confident as she sounded to Jennifer.

For his part, Lucas was already passed out in his father's armchair, snoring loudly. Byron suspected that he'd been so sleep-deprived the last couple of days, having some friends to watch his back must have been a load off.

Mary was flipping through an old paperback from a dusty bookshelf by the television, but it couldn't hold her interest. She was too anxious about what might happen tonight, if anything.

"So," she said, ambling over toward the big back window where Byron was set up. "That's an interesting name! Byron, I mean. Where'd your mom come up with that?"

Byron didn't look away from the window. "Lord Byron! He was a romantic poet, my mom's favorite. She loves poetry."

"Oh! Really cool. I love to read. I'll have to check him out. So long as we don't, you know, get murdered tonight."

Byron finally turned to look at Mary. He seemed delighted that she was interested. "My mom has a bunch of his books, actually. Really old ones, too! You can totally borrow them. If we don't, you know, get murdered."

"I'd like that a lot!" said Mary, already turning away so Byron wouldn't see the half smile spreading across her face.

After a couple more hours had gone by and nothing came scuttling through the fields to terrorize them, everyone was starting to feel exhaustion creep in. Byron was beginning to wonder if they'd really accompany him outside when midnight came around. They'd all been through so much already. Maybe it really was too much to ask them to hunt down the monsters hunting them.

Soon, everyone besides Byron was asleep. The television had been left on, and some infomercial was playing in the background. Byron didn't mind. He appreciated the background noise.

He sighed. They still desperately needed proof. He couldn't just let what happened to Bev happen again. Maybe this had been the wrong move, but he didn't know what else to do. Byron checked his watch and saw that midnight was fast approaching. He hoped one or two of the others would rouse and join him in the hunt, but he'd go alone if he had to. For Beverly.

He'd just gotten to his feet when he caught a flash of movement outside. The long, graceful form of a deer in the fields outside.

Byron gasped. Even from this distance he could see the creature had an unnaturally round, pale face. It reflected the moonlight like a sickly beacon. Byron could feel the humanlike eyes staring at him, even from this distance.

It was ambling back and forth in the grass in front of the farmhouse, moving in no real hurry. Behind it, Byron caught movement as more figures made their way through the cornfield toward the house. And not just deer. There was a shambling scarecrow, its boneless body rocking in the dark. And there—an impossibly tall figure glided through the stalks, capped in the unmistakable shape of a wide-brimmed hat.

They were coming for them. *All* the monsters were coming!

Byron turned to warn the others, ready to raise the alarm.

"Guys! Wake up—" he started, but as his eyes adjusted to the darkened room, he found his voice had abandoned him.

Standing over Rebecca as she slept was the sagging, rotten outline of a person. Its pale skin was splotched with gray, even in the shadows. And it wore a long mass of black fabric that was furry with rot.

The creature had the giant head of a crow.

This head tilted inquisitively in his direction, its white eyes finding his own.

"EVERYBODY RUN!" Byron screamed. Instantly, the room was thrown into chaos.

Mary was up first. Upon seeing the withered bird monster, she shrieked as loud as she could, scrambling back from her sleeping bag on the floor. The creature was reaching for Rebecca with its horribly long arms when a flash of light flared brightly in its face. The creature recoiled and cawed in irritation as Byron advanced with his camera.

"Get out of here, you creep!" he shouted, then took another photo. The flash was blinding in the enclosed space of the living room. The creature stepped backward, its long rotten arms raised in a defensive position over its face. Still advancing, Byron fired off a third shot. This time, the bird monster screeched in fury and an instant later disappeared *into* the wall, plunging through the surface as if it were a vertical pool of water.

They were alone again, but who could say for how long?

"If I hadn't turned around when I did, it would have . . ." Byron trailed off, his hands trembling around the camera.

"That was the thing I saw in the hideout!" Rebecca sobbed. "It found me!"

Lucas was already grabbing up their bags and tugging on his boots. "We have to go. It could come back at any time."

Byron shook his head. "It's not alone. More of those monsters are outside. They've *all* come for us."

Suddenly, the television started flipping through stations on its own. The volume rose as it settled on a dead channel, filling the room with noise and static.

"This is what happened when the deer attacked my house." Kyle stared into the glowing square of the television screen with wide eyes.

"But what is it doing?" Jennifer asked. "Is it calling them?"

"The same thing happened with my radio when the man in the hat appeared in my room," Byron said. "It went haywire just like this."

"We. Do not. Have time for this," Lucas said sternly.

Outside, more deer had congregated in the field, staring intently through the window. It almost looked like they were watching the TV set.

Through the static, everyone heard a strange whispered voice, just barely discernible.

"Please . . . BCON . . . Radio . . . I'm . . . sorry . . . They're . . . coming . . . Turn . . . it . . . off!"

Byron's blood ran cold. He recognized that voice. He'd been listening to it recount scary stories for years. It was the voice of Alan Graves.

"We have to get out of here!" Rebecca shouted. Her eyes were on the approaching monsters that were massing in the backyard.

A knocking sounded through the house. Something was pounding on the back door. Dark shapes swayed in front of the living room windows as the creatures reached the house.

"I am not getting that," Mary said.

"We can sneak out the front," Lucas whispered. "Let's just hope that most of them are grouped in the back." He grabbed a set of car keys hanging in the hallway.

"My dad took his car out of town," Lucas said shakily, "but there's an old junker beside the house that I've been repairing for years. It'll run. I've . . . definitely seen it run before."

Mary tried her best not to see the doubt in his eyes. As the monsters advanced on the isolated farmhouse, the group prepared to flee.

CHAPTER NINETEEN
GETAWAY CAR

All the noise seemed to be coming from the back of the house, and Lucas wanted to keep it that way. If they could just buy a couple of minutes, he was nearly positive he could get the old car running. Technically, it had run before—just not very well. But maybe it could get them far enough away from the Weaver farm that they could run the rest of the way to safety.

Everyone was crouched by the front door. Lucas rested his hand on the doorknob, preparing to whip it open.

"When I count to three," he said, "everybody run as fast as you can to the car. It should be unlocked. I've never worried about anyone stealing the old thing."

Jennifer held out her hand expectantly as she said, "Sounds like a plan, but I'm driving. I'm the oldest one here."

Lucas gazed at her upraised palm for only a second before dropping the keys into his pocket.

"Sorry, Jennifer, but I'm the only one who can get that car moving. It's gotta be me."

Jennifer frowned, but said nothing.

"Okay, everyone," Lucas whispered, "on the count of three. One." The group all looked at one another briefly, every face a mask of fear.

"Two."

Byron gripped his knapsack straps a little tighter. Mary held her heavy flashlight aloft like an oversized club.

"Three!"

Lucas tore open the front door to reveal an empty yard. The group burst out toward the side of the house, sprinting around the corner. Mary spotted the old car right away, a rusted hulk in the distance. They'd only just started for it when Lucas thrust a hand in front of everyone, stopping them dead in their tracks.

One of the mutant deer hopped up on top of the car. It shifted from one hoof to the other, the metal of the car roof denting and bending under its weight. As they watched, its pale moon face slowly swung in their direction. It looked from one kid to the next, a slow smile spreading across its waxy visage.

Byron gasped in shock, the breath leaving his lungs as forcefully as if he'd been struck.

No. No, it couldn't be . . .

He recognized that face.

He screamed, turning his head, his eyes clamped shut.

"I can't! I can't look at it!"

"What is it, Byron?" Jennifer said, still watching the creature for any sudden movements.

"It's Bev . . ." he whispered, just barely choking back a sob. "It has *Beverly's* face!"

The creature's pale skin and long hair were definitely Beverly's, but any emotion or humanity had long since disappeared from her face.

The Beverly deer hopped down to the muddy earth. It moved slowly, almost playfully, as it advanced toward them. Its jaw worked back and forth, then dropped open, revealing an enormous black hole of a mouth. As the group watched in horror, a thin and delicate arm emerged from within the gaping portal, clawing its way free.

Suddenly, something hit the monster in the face with an ineffectual thwack, before dropping to the ground.

Kyle had thrown the ziplock bag of trail mix at the monster as hard as he could.

"Had to try," he said, then took a step back.

Before anyone else could react, Mary rushed forward, waving her arms back and forth.

"I'll distract it. Get the car going!"

The long arm reaching out of the monster's throat lashed through the air, elongating disturbingly. It shot out toward Mary.

With a scream, Mary dropped to the ground, dodging the creature's grasp. Then she pushed herself up and took off running as fast as she could into the field. A second later, the deer followed after her.

Mary bolted for the relative safety of the cornfield. If she could get there before the deer caught her, she'd be able to hide among the stalks and buy the rest of the kids time to get the car going. Without a moment to lose, she reached the overgrown backyard and plunged into the field.

The creature followed close behind, the grotesque arm protruding from its throat, swiping at her hair and narrowly missing her.

Suddenly, she was surrounded by tall whispering cornstalks.

Mary pushed through several rows, staying low to avoid being seen. Behind her, she heard the Beverly deer following, sifting through the corn with its long arm. As long as she stayed ahead of the monster, she was certain that she could keep herself oriented and make it back to the road. Hopefully, Lucas and the others were already in the junker and she'd hear it roar to life at any moment.

Before long, the noise of her pursuer was far behind her. Mary found herself following one of the eerie rows farther into the field, until it opened up into a small clearing. She clicked on her flashlight and cast it back and forth, inspecting the area. She was fairly confident that she could no longer hear the monster stumbling after her. The cornfield was completely silent, aside from the rustling of the stalks in the night breeze.

All Mary had to do now was bide her time and circle back toward the road. She took a moment to catch her breath, resting her hands on her knees with her head bowed.

This must be the worst month in a new town anyone has ever experienced, Mary thought.

Then, a rustle. Light, cheerful laughter rang out across the empty clearing. Mary looked on in horror as across the empty space, a shape stepped into view. "Oh no," Mary said as recognition washed over her like a cold wave. The person stepping into the clearing was *her*, but horribly distorted. Her features stretched and undulated, shifting across the creature's skull as she watched. Slowly, the eyes, nose, and mouth squelched into the appropriate spaces on her face. It looked at her with mismatched eyes and smiled.

Mary's double had found her.

CHAPTER TWENTY
THE ESCAPE

Mary had only just disappeared into the corn when the grotesque animal went after her. All the rest of the group could do now was get the car running before any other monsters found them. They had no way of knowing if the creatures had made it into the house. Perhaps they were moving through it toward the front yard right this moment.

Lucas thought briefly of the crow-headed witch that had attacked them. If Byron hadn't turned at exactly the right time, it might have snatched Rebecca away before anyone had even known. Even now, it was probably still lurking around, ready to melt through the ground and grab their ankles. Who knew when any of them would suddenly appear?

Jennifer put a hand on his shoulder. "Lucas!" she said firmly. "C'mon, we gotta move!"

Lucas nodded, coming to. A few feet away, he saw that Rebecca was comforting a rattled Byron. The boy looked on the verge of a panic attack.

Seconds later, they were all cramming themselves inside the old car and Lucas was fumbling to get the key into the ignition. Rebecca, Kyle, and Byron had jumped into the back seat, while Jennifer sat beside him. They'd have to make room to squeeze in Mary, but they should all fit.

Lucas turned the key. The engine made a noise somewhere between a sneeze and a hoarse, grinding wail. He tried it again, but with a gentler touch, and the results weren't much better. All around, the shadows seemed to be closing in. The wind blew the cornstalks surrounding the car with an ominous whispering.

"C'mon, c'mon!" Kyle pleaded from his place in the back seat. "Start it!"

"I'm trying as best as I can!" Lucas yelled.

"Do I have to get out and push?!" Jennifer said.

"Just give me a minute . . ." Lucas said.

As he turned the ignition again, his eyes flashed up to the rearview mirror. Lucas gasped.

He nearly hadn't seen it emerging from the cornfield. Behind them, a man-shaped figure loomed, clothed in a variety of brightly colored garments. And its face was covered by an awful burlap sack.

"No, no, no," Lucas moaned. "Not the scarecrow. Not now!"

"What IS that thing?" said Rebecca, fascinated.

Lucas turned the key again and again, pumping the gas as he did. All the while, he kept an eye on the living scarecrow as it slowly shambled toward the car.

Amid the confusion, the car radio clicked on with a dull glow and the noise of static filled the car.

"Oh no—look!" Rebecca yelled. She pointed toward the edge of the house.

From around the corner, a tall figure in a long black coat emerged, its face a shadow under its wide-brimmed hat. But even from here, they could all see the monstrous grin that stretched beneath. "It's the Stranger," Byron said. "We have to get out of here, NOW."

Their panic growing every second, all the assembled kids watched as both the scarecrow and the Stranger got closer.

The scarecrow was the first to reach the car, and Kyle screamed as it slouched forward and peered through the rear windshield. Movements he had thought were the wind whipping the scarecrow's clothes were actually squirming motions from underneath. Long, spidery legs poked through gaps in the cloth, and a long chitinous arm ending in a pincer pierced the rough burlap of the thing's face.

As Mr. Sackhead put two gloved hands down on the trunk, the engine finally caught and came to life with a roar. Byron, still screaming, raised his camera and took several pictures of the creature's writhing mask.

"Punch it!" Jennifer yelled.

Lucas stamped on the gas pedal. The car lurched forward, and for a moment the painted eyes on the burlap sack almost seemed to glare at him. The scarecrow gripped the trunk tightly with its gloved hands as the car gained speed.

"Seat belts!" Lucas shouted, snapping his own into place.

As the car sped toward the back of the house, the motion pulled at the scarecrow's body. Parts of it fell away to reveal strange oversized insect limbs and swarms of maggots, but it wasn't enough to stop Mr. Sackhead. Lucas put the car in reverse and rocketed them backward—toward the cornfield—but the monster pulled itself up, clinging to the back windshield. It reared back with its right arm, preparing to smash the glass.

Lucas lifted his foot off the gas and slammed it back down on the brake. Instantly Mr. Sackhead was thrown backward, smashing through stalks until it landed in the wet and furrowed earth. The scarecrow all but exploded, its cloth body bursting open and spraying insects and worms in all directions. It moved weakly for another moment before lying still in the dirt.

The car radio clicked off on its own, and the car was filled with silence.

"Somehow, I don't think that's enough to get rid of it for good," Lucas said. "Is everyone okay?"

A chorus of shaky yeses sounded.

Glancing back at the house through the rearview mirror, Lucas saw the Stranger standing as still as a statue, just grinning at the car.

"Mary is still out there," Byron said. "We gotta find her!"

"Spoke too soon!" exclaimed Jennifer. "Look!"

Everyone's attention was drawn to a small form making her way out of the corn, stepping around the remains of the scarecrow. Awash in the red glow from the rear lights, Mary looked as if she had been in a bad fight. Her sleeve was torn and there was a cut over her right eye, but otherwise she seemed okay.

She rushed forward and all but dove into the back seat. "We gotta go!" Mary said. "Those deer things were right on my heels!"

"Say no more," Lucas replied as he put the car back into drive. "I think we've done enough monster hunting for one night."

Narrowing his eyes, he aimed right for the creature in the hat who still stood in their path.

"Out of our way, ugly!" Kyle screamed.

The car accelerated toward the imposing figure.

"Brace yourself!" Lucas yelled, and everyone prepared for the impact.

But just as the car would have plowed into the monster, he seemed to rise up and past the windshield, disappearing out of view as it roared past him.

"What just happened?" Jennifer asked in a stunned voice. "Where did he go?"

"Let's . . . try not to worry about it," Rebecca replied.

As the car made its way down the long road leading back to town, the Weaver farm shrank away in the rearview mirror.

CHAPTER TWENTY—ONE
NOT SO FAST

The car weaved across the road as Lucas struggled with the wheel. He'd had some practice driving before, but only with his dad in the passenger seat, making sure he didn't smash into one of the massive trees that bordered their property.

He was trying his best to keep the wheel steady, but everyone was still understandably panicked by their encounter.

Voices crashed over and against one another in an unintelligible jumble.

"Can everyone please be quiet?!" Lucas shouted.

The headlights swung across the empty road, highlighting every crack and pothole in their path.

"That was TOO close," Byron muttered from his place in the back seat.

"Yeah, you think?" Jennifer said, adjusting her seat belt. "We almost died for a bunch of pictures!"

"And all of those monsters are still out there," said Rebecca.

"She's right, unfortunately," Lucas said. "I've seen the scarecrow pull that disintegrate-into-bugs trick before. He came back like it was no big deal."

He scanned the woods for any possible monsters waiting to leap into the path of their speeding vehicle. After a while, though, when no attackers emerged, the car full of kids fell quiet. Only the sounds of the engine and the wind buffeting the windows blanketed them.

It was almost a shock when Mary suddenly spoke.

"Where are we even going?" she said. "I don't want to lead those things back to my parents."

"Police, right? It's definitely time to go back to the cops," Lucas said.

"Definitely," Jennifer agreed, a hint of optimism seeping into her voice for once. "All in all, we got what we came for. Byron snapped off a couple pictures of the scarecrow, as well as that awful bird-headed thing. If they turn out, then we've got some definitive proof."

"But that doesn't help us in the long run," Rebecca said. "Those things will still be after us. Why is this happening, and how do we stop it?"

"What connects all of our encounters?" Byron said. "I've been thinking. Not only do the monsters seem to mess with electronics like radios, televisions, and phones, but they match the exact descriptions of creatures from the Alan Graves show! And I'm positive that the voice from the TV tonight was him, too."

Mary nodded. "Alan Graves," she said quietly. "I heard part of his show on the radio as my parents and I were driving into town. We saw the radio tower on the peak at the far end of town."

Suddenly, Jennifer caught a flash of movement in the rearview mirror. Something big and dark rose from behind the car, torn fabric fluttering in the breeze. One moment the road behind them was an empty, dark expanse. The next, something was crawling up onto the trunk and then the dented roof of the car.

"What was *that*?" Rebecca moaned, alternating between peering out the back of the car and straining her neck trying to see out of the passenger window.

"Can't be good, right?" Lucas exclaimed, not looking away from the road.

Kyle's face was inches from the back window when something swung down from above. Suddenly, he was inches away from the upside-down face of a gigantic crow. Its head twisted back and forth as it peered in at him. He yelped, pulling away, but even as he did, he noted that there was something artificial about the black-feathered head. Subtle stitches connected fleshy seams, like the stuffed animals he'd seen once in West Virginia. He remembered the word his parents had used to describe them: taxidermized. He and his parents had driven out that way a couple of years ago and had ended up stopping in a strange little gift shop, full of oddities. There'd been so many of the dead but lifelike animals mounted on the walls and propped up around the shop.

Aside from the glint of life in the white eyes, he would have said this, too, was some kind of monstrous taxidermy.

The bird's head pulled out of sight again as the thing on top of the car shifted its position.

"It's on top of the car," Kyle whispered. "It just looked at me through the window——"

Suddenly, he was interrupted by a pale, withered hand that thrust through the roof of the car, right between Lucas's and Jennifer's heads.

Everyone screamed, throwing the car into chaos. Lucas did his best to dodge the swipes of the monstrous appendage while also keeping the car from crashing. The old junker swung from one side of the road to the other.

Rebecca curled into a ball in the back seat, while Byron stared in fascination at the point where the arm entered the car. Instead of ripped fabric and jagged metal, it was as if the roof was a pool of water that the creature had dunked its arm through.

The car weaved a dangerous path across the road, threatening to drift into the bordering pine trees at any given moment. Jennifer bashed at the arm with her flashlight, but all she succeeded in doing was loosening a seam in the creature's flesh. Small tufts of rotten-smelling sawdust fell out of the drooping hole in the flesh. They fell into the car like rancid snow, stirred into the air by the frantic motion of the monstrous arm.

Byron dug through into his army-green canvas backpack, then pulled out his ungainly camera. The arm had found Rebecca's leg and was locked in a death grip. It was only a matter of moments before it dragged her from the vehicle. Checking that the film was firmly in place and the flash was on, Byron unbuckled his seat belt and rolled down the window, then thrust his head and torso out into the cold night air.

The crow's face turned to him as he did, its white eyes blinking curiously. Byron took aim and pressed the shutter button.

Instantly, the dark night was filled with a blinding-white light. The thing on the roof screeched in shock and outrage, and then the cry was suddenly cut off. Byron blinked a couple of times, regaining his sight, and realized that the creature was gone. Carefully, he pulled himself back through the window.

"Is it gone?" Rebecca asked, rubbing her leg. In the place where the bird woman had grabbed her, a deep purple bruise was developing in the shape of her outstretched fingers.

"For now," Byron said. He buckled his seat belt again, but kept the camera close. "I guess it really hates bright light."

"Are we almost to town?" Jennifer asked. "I feel like we've been driving for hours."

Lucas frowned. "You're right. The drive isn't usually this long. Monster attacks aside, we should have seen *some* buildings by now, instead of just . . . trees."

Jennifer grimaced. "Something's really wrong here."

As if on cue, the engine suddenly started making an ominous chugging sound.

"Oh no, no," Lucas said. "Not now! C'mon, please don't cut out on us."

He rubbed the dashboard with as much compassion as he could muster, but in another moment the engine coughed and died, and the car rolled to a stop at the side of the road.

Now true silence filled the car. Lucas tried the ignition over and over, but nothing happened. They were stranded.

"We should move," Jennifer said. "We don't know how close those things are."

"She's right," Rebecca said. "Lucas, give it up. We gotta go." The girl grabbed her knapsack and unbuckled her seat belt. "Looks like we've got a little walk ahead of us."

CHAPTER TWENTY—TWO
LOST

They'd been walking for ten minutes by Byron's estimation, and he'd still seen no signs of civilization. He swung his flashlight beam back and forth across the road, trying to watch for monster attacks from both sides at the same time. The group traveled in a rough line, each with their own flashlight pointed toward the empty road ahead or behind them, or the woods to their left and right.

"Just a little farther," Lucas said. "We're probably just underestimating how long the road back into town is."

Whether he was trying to convince the others or himself, it was hard to say.

Byron nudged Mary to get her attention.

She turned to look at him with a neutral expression. "What is it?"

"Are you okay?" he asked. "You've been quiet since all that stuff at the farm. That was brave of you, by the way. Luring the deer out of the way. I just . . . I couldn't . . ."

Mary shrugged. "It was nothing. I lost the thing and circled back. Luckily, those things seem really dumb." She patted him on the shoulder. "I'm fine."

Mary gave him a smile, but there was a strange coldness behind it.

"If you say so," Byron muttered, not at all reassured.

Another twenty minutes passed in silence as the group tried their best not to panic. "We definitely should be in town by now," Jennifer said, panning her light over the woods, searching for the waxy, pale faces of the deer.

From the back of the group, Rebecca gasped. "Guys," she said. "They're behind us. Don't stop moving."

Everyone immediately stopped moving. One by one, they all turned their lights behind them and saw that they were indeed being followed. Several of the human-faced deer were keeping pace with them, their eyes shining in the shadows of the trees. As the group stopped, so did the deer.

"What are they doing?" Jennifer asked. "Why aren't they attacking?"

"It feels like . . ." Byron began. "Like they're herding us down the road. Doesn't make me feel great about what might be at the end."

More grinning, malformed faces emerged from the trees. After the first deer had been spotted, it was like the rest no longer saw the need to hide.

"Let's just keep moving," Lucas said. "What else can we do?"

"They're moving us somewhere," Jennifer said. "I don't like it."

The group traveled silently, keeping their flashlights trained on the deer watching from the tree line. Unlike with the crow creature, the light didn't seem to have an effect. Byron took a couple more snapshots, wondering if he'd ever have a chance to show anyone his hard-won proof.

Rebecca noticed that the trees that lined the road were looking stranger, more skeletal. Several were covered with a weird, pale kind of vine twisting around the trunk and limbs.

It wasn't long before they saw the signs of their destination.

In the near distance, a red light throbbed against the sky in a steady rhythm. They were heading directly for it, the road curving and pitching sharply uphill. Soon they could make out the steel struts of the radio tower and the crimson light suspended within. Beneath it rested a squat, square building.

The tower's red glow revealed four giant metal letters mounted to the front of the building, slowly succumbing to rust: BCON.

A chill crept over Byron. BCON Radio Station. It felt right, in a nightmarish fashion. It was the thread connecting all the supernatural horrors of Beacon Point.

"None of this geography makes sense," Jennifer said shakily. "We weren't anywhere near the station. How are we at the peak?"

"No point in worrying about it now," Rebecca said. "At the very least, if we survive, maybe we'll finally get some answers."

CHAPTER TWENTY-THREE
BCON RADIO

Byron was the first to reach the heavy double doors set into the front of the squat building, but the walls around the door frame gave him pause. Whatever paint had once covered them had long ago been worn down to reveal the dusty, chipped brickwork beneath. The stones looked not just old . . . but ancient. Just how old *was* this building?

He gave a quick look over his shoulder. The deer formed a line across the forest road, blocking all hope of turning back. They had no choice but to enter the building.

Byron tried the doors, half expecting to find them locked or jammed, but they swung open easily.

"Of course," he whispered.

"C'mon, everyone inside," Jennifer said. She ushered the group in, keeping a watchful eye on the deer until everyone else had entered. Once they were inside the station, she slammed the doors shut behind them. There was a bulky dead bolt lock set into the doors, and she snapped it into place. Lucas and Rebecca dragged a torn, cobwebby sofa in front of the doors for extra measure. They were secure against the army outside, but it did little to help with what awaited them here.

The group stopped and listened. There were no sounds of approaching footsteps, no strange monster noises. The building was dead silent. Jennifer peered out one of the front-facing windows and confirmed what she had suspected. The deer hadn't moved an inch. They stared toward the building.

"What IS this?" Lucas muttered.

"Well, Lucas," Jennifer said, "looks to me like a decrepit old radio station with six unlucky people stuck inside, driven there by the very monsters they tried to hunt. Does that cover it?"

"Wish I hadn't asked," he muttered.

The lobby looked fairly normal, if old and disused, with a long desk facing the doors that was presumably for a receptionist. To the right of this desk, a hallway stretched into darkness. A large potted plant rested in the corner, but it had long ago shriveled and died. In fact, everything in the space appeared run-down. Cobwebs stretched over the walls, and dust coated the surfaces. No one had stepped inside this building for many years.

"Wait, there's gotta be a phone here, right?" Kyle said. "We can call for help!"

Then he warily eyed the dark of the hallway to the right. It looked like a cavernous throat stretching, just waiting for them to step inside so it could swallow them whole.

"If we have to explore this creepy old radio station, so be it," Jennifer said. "But I am NOT exploring unarmed." With that, Jennifer marched over to the corner where several wooden chairs were sprawled haphazardly. Grabbing one up, she lifted it over her head and, in one fluid motion, smashed it to the ground. Seconds later, she had a short wooden club clutched in both hands, the remains of a chair leg. "I'd like to see one of those ghoulies get me now."

"Make sure to keep your flashlights handy as well," Rebecca said. "Who knows when that bird thing will come back?"

The group of kids huddled together as best they could, their flashlights and weapons in hand. Slowly, they started to move into the rest of the building.

Byron stuck to the back of the group with Mary, watching their rear. Occasionally he turned and swung his flashlight in a loose semicircle over the hallway behind them, but each time he revealed only a dirty, dust-covered floor and water-stained walls.

Byron glanced in Mary's direction. Ever since the chaos at the farm, she'd been weirdly quiet. Maybe she was traumatized. He frowned at her scratches and torn clothes. Mary had said she'd gotten away from the chasing deer, but he wondered if perhaps more had happened in the corn than she was letting on.

"Hey," he said. "Seriously—are you all right? You've been so quiet." Mary said nothing, but he could tell she was listening. He paused to scan the hall again, but everything was dead quiet, aside from the shuffle of many shoes on the linoleum floors.

"I know we haven't known each other very long," he said, facing forward again, "but you can talk to me. We've gotta have each other's backs."

Byron turned to look at Mary and found that she'd stopped a couple of steps back from the group and was staring back down the hallway they'd just traversed.

"Mary, do you see something?" Byron whispered. He peered for any signs of movement as he stepped closer.

"No," Mary said, turning to face him. "And I'm not Mary."

Byron raised his flashlight to her face and screamed. Mary's face was melting from her skull, succumbing to gravity like a hunk of old gum. The features beneath were monstrous. One newly revealed eye bulged from its socket and glared hatefully at Byron and the others, who were all now turning to see what the commotion was about. As the face of Mary's doppelgänger dropped to the dusty linoleum, the flashlight beam shone on a wicked sickle of a mouth. It grinned around countless needlelike teeth.

"What's wrong, Byron?" a warped voice rasped. "Don't you recognize me? Aren't we going to be frieeeendss, Byron?"

The creature that had been masquerading as Mary took one step forward, then another. The group screamed as one and scrambled into the waiting darkness of BCON Radio.

CHAPTER TWENTY—FOUR
INTO THE NIGHTMARE

Everything was thrown into chaos. The kids ran down the decrepit halls of BCON Radio, with the Mary thing close behind.

"Don't run from your friend Maaaaary," it called out mockingly, its eerie voice closing the distance with shocking speed.

Jennifer had fallen to the back of the group of fleeing kids. She knew it would only be a moment before the horrific double caught up with her. *The babysitter has gotta protect the kids*, she thought. Taking a deep breath and tightening her grip on the chair leg, Jennifer stopped and turned—facing off against the approaching monstrosity.

She took grim pleasure in the look of surprise on the doppelgänger's gruesome face.

"I am tired"—Jennifer said, bringing the chair leg up over her right shoulder—"of being CHASED."

Jennifer screamed the last word as she swung at the monster's head with all her might. The bludgeon connected and the shock of the impact shot up her arm like lightning, jangling her nerves all the way up to her shoulder. A hollow *thock* reverberated off the dusty walls of the hallway.

The Mary thing was knocked off its feet, colliding with the floor and sliding backward.

Jennifer looked on in shock. She couldn't believe that had worked!

Suddenly, a hand grabbed her sleeve. She jumped in surprise, but it was only Byron.

"Great swing," he said, "but we gotta go!"

Even as they both turned to catch up with the others, his eyes never left the slumped form of the creature. The Mary thing was twitching. It was only a matter of time before it was up and after them again.

The group ran down the seemingly never-ending hallways. Doors began to appear, but every one they tried was locked.

Behind them, Mary's warped voice rose again in a horrific cackle. It wasn't far behind.

"What are we going to do?" yelled Rebecca.

"I have absolutely no idea," Lucas responded in a panic, "but whatever it is, we better do it fast."

From the opposite direction came the noise of footsteps.

"Oh no," Byron said. "Don't tell me . . ." He swung his flashlight down the hall.

The man in the wide-brimmed hat strolled toward them, his long coat brushing the floor. As they watched in terror, the monster reached up and plucked the hat off his head, placing it gently against his chest. It was a strange gesture—polite and delicate—belying the nightmare of a face that had been revealed.

The creature's visage was a smooth expanse of wrinkled white flesh. He had no eyes or nose that they could see, just an enormous smile that stretched from one corner of his head to the other. His dark teeth glinted inside that tight red smile.

Cornered on both sides, the group didn't know what to do. They were just beginning to panic when one of the hall doors opened and a familiar face poked out.

"Quick, in here!" Mary said. "Hurry!"

The group was too shocked and desperate to do anything but comply. Mary opened the door a little more to allow them entry, before quickly slamming it shut and locking it. A moment later they'd barricaded the exit with some old chairs and a table, though the hallway outside remained suspiciously quiet.

"Are you . . . are you the real Mary?" Byron asked.

The girl nodded gravely. "Hard to prove, I know, but I've only seen one of those things so far."

"How in the world did you make it here on foot?" Jennifer asked. "We drove for miles to reach this place."

Mary shook her head. "I'm not totally sure, to be honest. I think time and space are a little funny here. When I ran into the cornfield to distract the deer, that *thing* was waiting for me. It almost got me, but I escaped and found myself on the road. When I never saw any sign of the car, I decided to start walking. Eventually, more deer appeared, but they didn't attack. They just sort of followed me here, to BCON Radio." She shuddered. "I've been wandering around ever since, trying to find the way out. The hallways have a way of twisting on you."

"Something's been pulling us here," Lucas said. "And now it won't let us leave until its little game is finished. But why? Why not kill us all?"

"It's like we've all been assigned a specific monster from those stories on the radio show," Rebecca said.

"Exactly," Byron said. He clicked on his flashlight and reached into his knapsack. Soon he pulled out the big notebook. "I think that something *here* is bringing all these creatures from Beacon Point history to life. Every monster we've seen tonight was talked about on the Alan Graves show. And in their presence, electronics seem to go defective. It's like they're picking up some strange transmission."

Byron flipped through the scrapbook. Newspaper clippings about strange deer were accompanied by scrawled writing—notes from specific episodes of the Graves show. Each accompanied by a specific date. As Byron scanned through more pages, Lucas saw notes on doppelgängers, mutant centipedes, the bird hag, living scarecrows, and other ominous figures, like the hat-wearing boogeyman that they'd just barely evaded.

"Well, if this place is causing the monsters," Mary said, "maybe there's some way we can stop them. Maybe someone led us here for a reason."

Lucas frowned. Something had changed in the room. He could see Byron's journal without the need of a flashlight. He glanced up to find they were all in some sort of large office storeroom. A dim redish light was now filling the room.

"Hey, where's that light coming from?" he whispered, looking around the space.

Slowly, they all turned. On the back wall, there was a simple wooden door; red light was leaking from the cracks in the frame. It bathed the group in its eerie glow.

"Was that there before?" Kyle asked incredulously.

"I'm not sure," Mary said. "But I think we're supposed to open it."

"For sure," Jennifer said. "I mean, I'm sure nothing bad will happen if we open the spooky door."

"I don't know that we have any choice," Mary said. "It's not like we can find our way back out. This isn't a normal building. The road led us all here. Same with the voice on the radio."

She crossed to the door. After a moment of contemplation, Mary turned to the others.

"I'm gonna open it," she said.

"If you're sure about that," Lucas responded, though he didn't look very confident in the decision.

"I'm sure," Mary said. "On the count of three."

"Who knows, maybe it's locked," said Rebecca.

Jennifer raised her chair leg; the others hoisted their flashlights like clubs.

"One," Mary said quietly. The others tensed up in anticipation.

"Two," she said, a little louder. She put her hand on the knob.

"Three!" Mary shouted as she tore the door open. The others jumped forward, ready to attack. But instead of attacking monsters, they found a simple stone staircase leading down. It was filled with the same dim red light, leaking upward from below. Peering down, Mary could see the edge of a stone room. The source of the glow was just out of view.

Suddenly, the door behind them wrenched open and the Mary thing was there. "Oh, my friends!" it crooned. "My friends!"

"Quick! Now!" Mary screamed. She and the rest of the kids crowded into the stairwell and slammed the door shut behind them. They clambered downward, trying not to listen to the creature behind them cackling on the other side.

CHAPTER TWENTY—FIVE
THE MACHINE

As he made his way down the crumbling stone steps, Byron took note of just how little of this made sense. The walls were made of rough stone bricks—much older and more solid than what would have been used in the construction of a small-town radio station.

Approaching the room at the bottom of the stairs, Byron switched off his flashlight. The others all followed suit. The crimson light that filled the space was more than enough to see by.

The first things that Byron noticed as he entered the massive underground chamber were the wires. Thick cables of various sizes crowded almost every available space, running along the floor and climbing the rough stone walls like strange vines. They disappeared into the ceiling before snaking off to various points in the upper parts of the radio station, Byron assumed. Huge bookshelves, loaded with ancient-looking tomes, lined the walls.

Looking around, Byron noticed a number of old papers and books stacked in piles that dotted the area. Picking up a document at his feet, the name Crawford Foley stood out. Byron was sure he'd heard that name somewhere before.

"This seems like a strange place for a radio show to be recorded—" Jennifer said. Huge speakers sat in all four corners of the room, facing the center. Red emergency floodlights hung from the ceiling, the source of the eerie light. Following the wires, Byron's eye was brought to the center of the wide chamber. All the cables seemed to begin there.

A massive oak desk was planted inside a red circle that had been painted into the floor. Surrounding it were steel boxes—a machine used to record or project audio, Byron assumed. And seated at the desk was an obscured figure, their back to the group.

"Uh, hello?" Rebecca said, trying not to let a tremble enter her voice. "Are you Alan Graves? We really need help. We're trapped here, and there are things after us. Hello?"

The figure didn't move. Their posture was slouched, their head resting on the desk as if napping in the world's most unwelcoming basement.

"Enough of this," Rebecca said, already stalking toward the slumped form.

"No, don't!" Lucas shouted.

But it was too late. As Rebecca tugged on the figure's shoulder, it slid from its spot on the desk and fell to the floor in a heap.

The kids all gasped. It was a corpse—a skeleton—its bones threaded with cobwebs. A large microphone sat propped on the desk on a tarnished steel stand. Surrounding it were more piles of papers, file folders, and photographs. Picking through the papers, Rebecca saw something familiar.

"Hey, check this out," she said. "It's the bird thing!" She waved a blurry Polaroid in the air.

"Are you sure?" Kyle said. "That looks like it could be anything, really. Just looks like a blurry bunch of smears."

"I'm sure it's my monster," Rebecca said, throwing the photo back on the pile. She had a feeling that all of theirs were here in one form or another, collected in these documents.

Lucas followed a thick cord that ran from the microphone to the machine beside the desk, which he now realized was turned on, as indicated by a glowing white light on the side.

"What's happening here?" Jennifer asked, stunned.

Then she realized that they were no longer alone in the claustrophobic basement.

"They're here!" Jennifer shouted. Various figures cloaked in shadow were pressed against the walls.

Jennifer and the others crowded around the desk in a chorus of screams. All the monsters that had been terrorizing them were there, manifested in the darkness.

The Crow Mother watched Rebecca closely, its white eyes trained on her, its long and snatching fingers twitching in agitation.

And there was Mr. Sackhead, slumped against the wall. Its painted eyes watched Lucas as long white worms dripped from its clothes onto the concrete.

Mary saw her doppelgänger, its true face revealed as a scaly, bug-eyed horror now protruding from the ruin of Mary's own face and body, the rotten yellow flesh contrasting with her own brown skin.

Byron glared at the Stranger, his wide coat dragging along the floor. The man hadn't yet replaced his wide-brimmed hat, and though he had no eyes to watch with, his toothy grin seemed aimed right at Byron. Byron took a step back and stumbled against the machinery, which seemed jarred to life.

Sparks flew across the stone floor, and the air filled with an ominous humming. The creatures advanced from all sides, but just as the kids thought there was nowhere to go, the monsters stopped short.

Byron looked down. His monster's feet stopped right at the circle of red paint on the floor.

"They can't cross over—" he realized. "Stay in the red circle! They can't pass through!"

As the machinery whirred into motion, the speakers in the corners of the room squealed to life.

The kids covered their ears as the air was filled with static. The noise seemed to drive the monsters into a fervor. They pressed on the air, desperate to penetrate the red circle, but it was like a physical barrier impeded them.

As Byron watched, the Stranger pushed his gloved hand hard, briefly budging past the circle before his arm was forcibly thrown back out.

"I don't think it's going to hold!" Mary shouted. "We need to get out of here!"

"Oh no, look!" Jennifer screamed. She pointed above them to a space near the high basement ceiling. Floating over their heads was a silhouette rendered in static. It flicked in and out of existence, its form glowing and shifting with white noise.

It had no discernible features, nothing aside from the outline of a person, but Mary got the impression that it was begging them for help. The static pouring out of the speakers suddenly cleared, resolving itself into a voice.

"Please . . . The . . . machine . . . The . . . wires . . . Cut . . . the . . . wires . . ." the mysterious voice said. "Please . . . free . . . me . . ."

The creatures were growing bolder. All four pushed on the invisible wall keeping the kids safe. "It said cut the wires!" Lucas screamed.

"Yeah, but should we listen to that glowing static guy?!" Kyle said.

"I really, really don't think we have a choice!" shouted Jennifer in response.

In a second, Mary had produced the knife from her bag and extended the blade. She fell upon the wires that ran from the machine to the wall and began sawing at one of the cables.

"They're almost through!" Rebecca screamed, scrambling atop the desk to avoid the filthy arm of the Crow Mother, now fully past the circle. It swiped at her face, just barely held back by whatever waning wards kept the horrors at bay.

Above them, the floating figure repeated its message about cutting the wires, and finally Byron understood.

The skeleton crumbled at their feet; the shape floating overhead; the voice on the radio. They were all the same.

"It's the radio host," he gasped. "It's Alan Graves!"

And as if in answer to that revelation, Mary held up a severed cable and screamed, "I did it!"

The machine surrounding the desk sparked and hissed and the red light blanketing the basement seemed to dim and then grow brighter.

But the monsters just continued their assault, growing ever closer.

"It's not enough," Rebecca said. "The machine is still running!"

"Enough of this!" Jennifer cried. Angling under the grasping hands of the crow creature, she slid to the central machine. Then she raised the chair leg and brought it down with a crunch—once, twice, three times.

On the third strike, the room filled with a horrible screeching. A shower of sparks rained over the kids, forcing them to cover their ears and close their eyes.

And then, as quickly as it had come, the static cut out and the room was silent.

Mary was the first one to look up. The room was now pitch-black. Switching on her flashlight, she drew it over the broken machinery. It was now a smoking, dented pile of metal on the floor, utterly ruined. A layer of chalky ash now covered the desk, the remains of the evidence that had been spread there. All gone.

The monsters, too, were gone. The basement stood empty, aside from the kids and the crumbled remains of Alan Graves's skeleton.

"Is it over?" Kyle asked, squinting into the basement.

"I think so," Lucas said. "I'm not totally sure what happened here, but that machine had something to do with it."

"I think Alan Graves, or whatever was left of him, needed our help," Mary said.

As they made their way up the stairs and back into the storeroom, Byron was almost completely unfazed to look back and see that the doorway they'd just come through was no longer there—instead, the room ended in a smooth, unbroken wall. He was the only one to notice.

Outside, it was early morning. The sun peeked through the trees and birds chirped cheerfully in the woods.

"It's like it never happened," Lucas said. "Did we hallucinate all that?"

Lucas had worked many tiring days, but an exhaustion like he'd never felt before now permeated his bones.

"Oh, it happened," Byron said. "I think we're all very lucky to be alive right now. And I think, somehow, Alan Graves saved us."

"I need a shower," Rebecca said, already walking down the road toward town.

"And a bed!" Jennifer added.

"And breakfast!" Mary exclaimed.

"Amen to that," Lucas muttered.

They trudged as one, back toward the suburbs of Beacon Point.

CHAPTER TWENTY-SIX
BACK TO NORMAL

Byron tipped his knapsack upside down and shook it much more violently than was strictly necessary, causing a rain of photos to cascade onto Mary's fuchsia-colored bedspread.

"C'mon, don't mess up my room," she said. "I just got it how I like it!"

She reached out to organize the scattered photos into a tidy stack. "My dad will be on me quick if we get it all disorganized."

Byron finished upending his backpack and nonchalantly tossed it in the corner.

"We'll clean up when we're done," he said. "Don't worry."

Rebecca picked up the stack of photos and held them up for everyone to see. The survivors of that horrible night at the BCON Radio Station had assembled in Mary's room to see how their work had turned out. By the looks of things, not well at all.

"These are all terrible," Jennifer said, squinting at a blurry patch of white on a field of dark. This more or less made up *all* the monster photos they'd taken that night.

"I don't know," Mary said. "Is that . . . can you make out a hand in this one?"

"I wish some of those papers from that creepy basement had survived," Rebecca said.

"If only we were so lucky," Jennifer said. "Alas."

After they'd made it back to town, each of the kids had tried telling their parents, their teachers, anyone who would listen about what they'd experienced over the course of that terrible night, but absolutely no one would take them seriously.

Mary's mom thought Mary had a great future as a writer, if she was making up ridiculous stories like that at such a young age. These photos had been their last hope, and the group had pooled their meager savings to get them developed.

Finally, they had arrived. Byron had been the one to pick them up, calling everyone together at Mary's house for the grand reveal. And now, nothing. Just squares of black with blurry colors smeared across their surfaces.

"Sorry, guys," Byron said. "I was taking them under situations of extreme stress. My life was in danger; you can't really blame me for having shaky hands." He flipped through the stack, looking for any that might have turned out. Eventually, he gave up and tossed the stack back onto the bed.

"So much for definitive proof," he said. "We risked our lives for nothing."

Lucas picked up a magazine from Mary's bedside table and

flipped through it without really reading it. "I wouldn't say that," he said. "It seems like we stopped the monsters from getting anybody else, at least for now. My scarecrow is just a scarecrow again. And we all became fast friends, right?" The rest of the kids groaned in mock anguish.

Mary's mom called up the stairs to let them know that dinner was ready. Her parents had been delighted to invite Mary's new friends over for dinner and a sleepover. The rest of the evening flew by in a blur of idle chatter about schoolwork, teachers, and how Mary was settling in.

The kids all ended up cocooned in sleeping bags draped in a rough semicircle around the living room TV, which rested in its giant wooden entertainment unit.

And though the others had groaned, Lucas couldn't help but be thankful for his new friends. As he drifted off to whatever dumb horror movie they were watching, he was comforted to be surrounded by others who had also experienced the scary things that lurked in Beacon Point. For now, they were safe.

He had no idea how long that'd last, but if the monsters did rear their ugly heads again, he'd have friends to back him up.

Byron, however, knew that the horrors unleashed at the radio station were just a sample of the paranormal forces that lurked here. He had an entire notebook full of stories to prove the point, spanning back centuries, and plenty of blank pages for new ones.

As he watched the flickering images on the television—fake monsters and fake blood—it was surreal to think of what he'd seen in the past month. Movies were tame in comparison. As he drifted off into an uneasy sleep on the floor, his friends laughing and talking all around him, it seemed for a moment like the screen flickered, breaking into patterns of static.

Just interference interrupting the picture, he thought.

Closing his eyes, Byron told himself that he hadn't seen a face staring out at them from the static, that it was just a product of his half-asleep mind.

And he hoped that the eyes he'd seen there wouldn't follow him into his dreams.

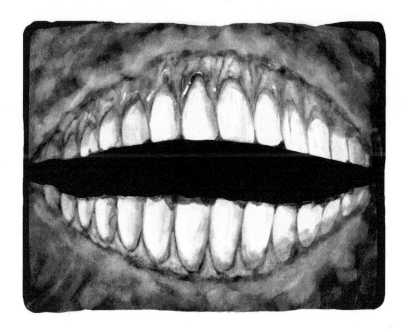

ABOUT THE AUTHOR

Trevor Henderson is a horror artist, illustrator, and author. Known for his terrifying internet cryptid creations—such as Siren Head, Cartoon Cat, and many others—he is also the illustrator of *Flicker* by Jed Shepherd. Trevor lives in Toronto, Canada, with his partner, Jenn Woodall, and their cat, Boo.